A Beacon in the Light

Austin S. Long

ISBN: 979-8-9919255-0-1 (paperback)
ISBN: 979-8-9919255-1-8 (ebook)

Note

Ely is a real city in Minnesota, as are the surrounding lakes and rivers. But their names are all that's shared with what is depicted here. Liberties have been taken with the region's true topography. With the exception of William's cabin, which is inspired by my own once owned on my Mother's side, (and has been transported in the novel from its true location off the shores of Big Sandy Lake to Burntside), the various homes, the camp, and all characters herein are works of fiction and are not intended to bear any resemblance to real places or real people, alive or dead.

A Beacon in the Light

William

CLOSE YOUR EYES and press the palms of your hands against them. Lightly. Or only enough for a bright halo of light to assert itself over your vision. Hold long enough and the light will bloom to blot it out entirely, and that's it: that's blindness. It's not a growing darkness. The dark is first to go behind the conflagration.

The doctor called it Retinitis Pigmentosa. He said, "It'll take his sight in a few years."

Mom gave me a weary smile when I looked at her. I didn't catch her expression before she changed it. Dad's is most often some impression of my own though, so I must have taken it alright. No one let much of anything show, and when we agreed in silence that it was okay, my father folded his arms and said, "What should we do now?"

We practiced saying it in the car with the radio off. It was raining outside with paths of it merging and roping out again on the window, and through a narrow thicket of eucalyptus trees were shifting bands of a gray and darkening horizon. The day drew down with a lid of fog twenty then ten feet off the ground and it was night before we got home. On the following morning my parents planned the next decade of my life. It was the kind of busy day that only comes after troubling news.

My mom rummaged through her old boxes brought down from the attic and stacked near the fireplace three or four high. She found her Polaroid and said for me to take pictures of things and people I like, and to keep from committing anything I don't to memory. She wanted to know what I'll remember long after I go blind; said that one day she'd ask about something in a photograph to test if I've done my diligence remembering. It seemed important to her that I never forget what she or Dad or what I looked like; nor the cabin, the lake, or my school. She warned that people tend to hold onto the worst things, and it became a daily routine for her to work only the best things into memory. She would ask, "Do you remember when Dad took you in the paddle boat across the lake and ran it into the trees and covered himself in spiders?" Or, "When the flames looked green in the fireplace? The stars and the moon like a dinner plate over the water?" Often, her voice would catch and she'd cover her mouth and go into another room for awhile.

I've neither photographed for or told her about this place: the Promontory over Little Bass Lake where an Eastern Cottonwood stands. The waves have taken the land from underneath it and its exposed roots twist into the impression of a hand that keeps the headland from total erosion. The canopy is lit up in the dusklight like fire, where a breath of wind plays through the leaves that whisper when they brush against each other. Lily steps where I do, through the knee-high sideoats.

Carved onto the black bark of the cottonwood is an old etching of a cross, and there are rusted tins you don't see in stores anymore buried in the clay near the roots. Otherwise, there's nothing to suggest the place has been visited by anyone in a long time. We lay out bath towels and sit. There are some hours left of the day, judged by the shadow of the Promontory that marks the time which has now touched the opposite shore where a berm of oak is reflected on the water like a waveform. The paling sky is spotless to the east, nothing to tell the eye of the miles between us and the horizon, and it looks like it's all painted on a canvas like what people used to think of the stars. With the cooling air comes a scattering of clouds from the west, whose shadows reveal the distances. Far off, a storm drags a column of rain across a hundred acres of land, narrow as a paintbrush, then dissipates as fast as it appeared.

A place like this is bound to be discovered by others. Then will come trails and campgrounds for its sake, then a name. Until that time the Promontory is kept close, secret. Talk of it going no further than the reach of a whisper.

The crickets fall silent as Lily tries to whistle something beside me. She's flipping through a book on native insects in her lap, turning the pages in some measure of the waves against the shore, perhaps subconsciously; much too fast to have read them, though. She must have gotten the book from the school library only to appeal to my interest. I talked with her about them one time only to fill the silence, and since then, we routinely trade stories of what we've seen in the wild. And just now, I've caught the sight of a huge wolf spider probing the edge of my bath towel with its forelegs. "Look," I whisper. Lily does, sucking in air like her head was about to be pushed under water. I laugh to sound brave. "It's okay, I don't think they bite."

"They do bite!" she says.

"Well, their bite isn't that bad. Look." I sit up and lean over to it, careful not to move the towel and scare it off. "Watch."

"Don't!"

I cup my hand over the spider and bring it up with a tuft of grass and some dirt. It goes stiff and I pluck it from my right hand into my left and hold it like an acorn in the tips of my fingers. Its body is hard and smooth. Lily has her hands over her mouth and her eyes are wide with fear and fascination. The wolf spider twitches with sudden determination to escape, its legs raking the empty air in a maze of spindly brown limbs. Lily lets out a little *yip*. She was an anxious knot of phobia when we first met. Afraid of the forest, of the water and darkness and storms and bugs, all bugs, especially spiders who spin strong webs to catch and keep leaves and twigs and those white calluses that hold the corpses of other bugs, or more spiders. It's all I've really given her, so far: a little bit of boldness to bring her out of fear of the world.

"Watch," I say, placing the spider on my arm. It crawls swiftly to my elbow before making its way to my shoulder. Without meaning it I shake it off me, but I'm quick to snatch it back from the ground and try over and over again until the sensation of its little legs stitching up and down my arms and neck is nothing to me. "You try."

Lily shakes her head, her ponytail coming loose and some of her tawny hair falls around her face.

"Just try."

"What if it bites me?"

"It won't," I say. "You might as well be a boulder or a tree stump for all it knows."

I take her hand and she pulls away at first but surrenders it eventually, then I place the wolf spider into it. She trembles but fights the urge to pull away while the spider dances up and around her arm then leaps like a frog from her shoulder onto the ground and scampers into the folds of the Cottonwood's bark. She shudders. "I hate spiders." I let go of her arm. "I only like pretty bugs," she says while scooting back to her spot. She breaks open the book again and I lie down on my back.

"You mean, you only like the harmless ones."

"I mean pretty ones. I hate roaches and they're harmless. Hyalophora Cecropia," she says, and holds the book out for me.

"What about it?"

"Look!"

I do. It's a true-to-size photo of a moth that spans most of the page. Blue-gray wings with a crimson body and submarginal lines. Eye-spots on the tips of its fore-wings. "It's dead," I tell her. "See how the wings are pinned open? A live one would have them open like this." I draw the shape with my finger over the page.

Lily closes it shut and leans away. She's silent for

a while. The crickets return before she says, "When you see something, you never have to look at it again, is that it?"

"Something like that."

"Then you better never forget what I look like."

I shrug. "How will you know if I do?"

"I'll just know. I'll know it like hunger."

"Well, never is a long time," I say. Then again, often in the night I walk around in the pitch dark inside my home or the woods nearby, and with nothing to see and that much less to recall of the minutes and the hours, time moves fast. Maybe I'll remember her face or maybe not, either case, "you'll change," I say. "You'll grow up and what I remember won't matter."

She scoots close again and leans over me. Her hair is like the bow of a violin – that precise range of colors from blonde to light brown. Her eyes are like the dark interior of rain clouds. The freckles on her face make Cassiopeia, make many constellations. "Just imagine me with wrinkles," she says.

"People change more than that. But I'll remember your voice."

She scoots back and looks out over the water. I think about kissing her all the time, but never imagine bringing it about by intention. It's always some contrived circumstance that forces us to kiss. Like an accident, tripping in such a way that our lips crash into each other. "My mom's voice sounds so different than when she was young." says Lily. "I don't think you'll recognize me by that."

"I guess not."

"Do you have to leave?"

"My mom says the city will be easier on me, but I don't think that's true."

"When?"

"Soon. I lie to the doctors about how bad it is, but they have tests. They can tell I'm almost blind in one eye. It's like looking through a doughnut of light. They say I won't be able to see at all by this time next year. I have to leave before winter. I think I'll be held back a grade," I say. For a time there's only the wind through the leaves and the water on the shore. It's getting cold.

"Two months left to make an impression on you," says Lily. An attempt at humor, I think.

The shadows are long now. The sun will set very soon. "We should go back," I tell her.

"Okay," she says, and we stand and she's looking down at my feet and clutching the encyclopedia to her chest. One of those moments passes its timeliness, that precise instant a bold act may be welcomed, but certainly isn't anymore. A loon calls somewhere, and she starts down the Promontory.

From the Cottonwood we cut north-east around the lakeshore, then direct east through an expanse of trees known by their pattern against the sky. Lily and I speak of nothing important. It's an hour of walking and the sun has set when we reach her house. There are no lights on inside. The windows are like dark sockets that stare right back at me. Lily stops well before the door and turns. "I'll see you tomorrow?"

"See you," I say. She makes a face. A slight smile, but there's more there than that. Disappointment?

A Beacon in the Light

What I do know is that if it all went white this second, her face as it is would impose itself over everything, forever. Within the spaces between trees and through the canopy, onto fallen leaves and the eye-spots on the wings of moths. I turn from her, embarrassed to stay or even to look back, and I step off the road into the woods. It's dark now, but I know the way back.

A semi-truck howls past. Its wake shakes the bushes and jostles the scarf from my neck. Moxie holds herself close to my side, stiff with nerves. She crosses her body over my left leg in a way to communicate that it's unsafe to go on. I urge her forward but she won't move, and neither do I have the confidence to cross without knowing if there's a jersey barrier or a simple grass median. Pineshire Way was a two-lane road when I left here, and in just two miles north it was no more than a footpath. Now, it's a highway, conveying vehicles with large tread lugs that slap down onto the pavement like rubber hooves. Another semi goes past and I turn from the road and bring Moxie around with the harness. She takes the lead and does her best to bring us through the berm of young oak we came through and back on the trail.

She's a city dog trained to avoid hazards like cars or trifficades or sprawled homeless on the sidewalk, and to find exits. But the hazards of the wilderness aren't framed in cautionary colors and orthogonal boundaries, and there are no exits or entrances but what she mistakes for them sometimes. The going is slow, less so after a week, but I'm afraid I've only trained her out of being an effective guide dog. After some months of this, the poor girl will never be able to work again.

With distance, the hiss of traffic fades behind the gentle pitter-patter of rainfall. It comes down in small, cold droplets that waft traces of iron from the soil and sweet rot from fallen tree stuff into the air. In Phoenix, the monsoons kick up so much dust that you can smell the rain long before it comes, if at all. But here the rain comes without much preamble, and this is so even if your eyes work.

Moxie pulls us around something blocking the trail. I flick my white cane at it; a puddle, half a foot deep. To my left emerges the sound of rain ticking on a metal roof. It's an old abandoned truck. Nineteen sixty-seven Chevy Longhorn rusted to the color of the clay it sits. I go to it and wave my hand over the engine compartment but there's nothing. The stubborn hazelnut tree that was growing there has since died in these twenty-some years.

It's an hour back to Burntside Lake. The time measured by the steps between one remembered thing and the next, such as the Longhorn, and, farther east, the wooden fence on a fringe marking some long-irrelevant border, the pickets jutting up unevenly from the clay like bottom teeth from retreating gums. Farther still, the water-smoothed white oak roots you could crawl under. Each of them *seen* as a sudden absence, like the backward crawl of words deleted from a white page, the pale ghost of them hanging there for a time, or for me, all time. But these memories drift unsupported without the travails to place them, without being where they fit, and I have tried to place them where they don't go. Even now they don't fit right. Too much has changed. That intricate and exposed root system, for example, has been discovered by an increasing number of people. I found the place littered with beer cans and broken bottles I'd be damned to ever bring Moxie through. Hatchets and pocket knives had been taken to the roots as well; overlapped scars and carvings covering them entirely.

For a quarter mile there's little I recall but for the road. Maybe it's a sense of timing or some other unreckonable detail, but I know exactly when to turn left onto the narrow drive to my old cabin. Grass thrives the length of it except where the tire grooves are. There are two homes that share the extended driveway: a black-wooded cabin to the left with rose bushes under the gable, and my own cabin with no such botanical considerations at the end of the path where it turns sharply to the right and sweeps down to the front door. The light of blindness has taken these forms, or has become nothing in comparison. Where the driveway turns, my white cane thwacks the rear tire of the moving truck parked at top of the hill, where down from it, sits my little pale-green cabin. I'm told it's since been repainted a more appealing shade of green, but why strain to imagine it any other way? It's a single-story with a porch that goes out over a steep fringe on stilts. A stone staircase a few paces from the front door cuts to the dock. About halfway down, the roots of an ash tree take the place of two steps. On the fringe cling raspberry bushes. It's too steep for bears and deer who would eat the berries, leaving birds who eat just a little, so there are always some left on the brambles, if you're willing to risk a swift tumble into the water, anyway.

Though it's raining, I don't supply it to my recollection of the lake. Without intention, I see the waters shimmering under a late sun, since I often returned home at such an hour. The shadows of waterfowl skirt the surface to the eastern shoreline where a narrow A-frame stands abandoned. Stood. It could be gone for all I know.

I begin down the grassy hill, slick with rain. The front door of my cabin swings open before I've reached it, its hinges articulating the presence of rust somewhere within them. It's Jessica. She calls for Moxie and slaps her legs. "Come on girl!" I try to put her there in the doorway, but the attempt only does her harm. It's always a struggle to keep from imagining her as another person. As someone I'd seen when I could – as my teachers who were her age, or worse, as Her. But fighting this impulse leaves nothing about Jessica that can compete. She is a ghost against the vividness of the cabin, the woods, the lake, and she always will be.

Moxie trembles and whines with excitement, but doesn't pull against the harness. "Good girl," I say, then to Jessica, "You're turning her into a pet."

"You've done that already. I'm just giving her a personality now," she says. My boots slide a bit on the grass when I stop in front of her. "Anyway, I need your help with something," she says before going back inside.

I pull my muddy boots off and set them on a

towel by the door. "Any surprises for me?"

"Some boxes in front of the fireplace."

The kitchen smells of earl gray deep in the wood. There's a small pantry to the left that presently holds the dog crate. I lay the harness and leash on top of it and lean the white cane against the wall under the light switch. In the living room and on the western wall is a gray-brick fireplace centered between two bedroom doors. On the opposite wall is a window eight feet across and four high, lacking the wooden muntins that would only obstruct the view of the lake; it's cobalt water so often the subject of dreams. Improbable waves in the throes of unnatural storms. A rowboat out there, and a man wrestling with the ores. Under the large window sits a driftwood table smoothed and waxed. Each Sunday morning was sat a plate of pancakes topped with melting pats of butter and cuts of bacon. The scent vaguely present in the recollection. A blessing. Forget alarm clocks. The smell of breakfast will do better, and the day through the window. Then at night the light of fire on the hearth and the dancing shadows to hypnotize you back to bed.

Have I returned only to steep in pleasant memories? Of course not, but I lost say over my mind long ago.

In the corner near my old room stands a Victrola. On the turntable a record spins without sound. The vinyl disc slows to reveal cursive letters over a dark orange label. Exactly as in a dream, it's only the essence and form of letters. No meaning at all. It seems I never bothered to read them. The Victrola was my mother's.

She'd play music from it sometimes and we'd pretend to be passengers on a ferry across Lake Superior, of which it shared its history.

"What goes there?" asks Jessica, suddenly behind me.

"A standing Victrola the size of a dresser. I think a lamp will do," I say. She must be looking at me now, observing. Where am I? Where in this place? Lost track. Drifted without involvement of the mind.

"Should we get a Victrola?" she asks.

"No, I don't think so."

"Wouldn't it be better if everything is as you remember? As you see it?"

"I don't see it."

The warmth of her draws closer, and the air shifts to accommodate her standing right beside me now. "It looks like you see it. You're looking right at it," she says.

"Am I?"

"You are. It's like it's there."

"It's not there."

"But most things are, right? The roads, the homes, even the trees that have only grown? You lead Moxie around more than she leads you."

"New growth. New roads, others abandoned. All the places I know well enough to find are in such a narrow scope anyway. It doesn't need to be exactly like it was. It's better if it isn't."

"What kind of scope?" she asks.

I turn to her. "Well, I know the way to Tucker's Tackle Supplies, if it's still there. I know the road to

Winton where I used to get Blue-moon ice cream. I know most places around the lake."

"What else?"

"I know the way to school. To camp."

"And?"

"And... to friends."

"Friends?"

"Yes, friends, and a girl."

"A girl now or a girl then?"

I wrap her up in my arms. She's small and malleable like a cat. Her shoulders are cold. "Is that why you came so soon? To see if I was running away with someone?"

"I came because you didn't want me to." She lays her head against my chest. "You can't buy a place in another State then fly off with a couple weeks' warning without suspicion."

"I jumped at the chance. It was automatic."

"And I'm happy for you. But why alone?"

"Alone, because I didn't know if it was safe here. I only got the place because the previous owner wanted to get away."

Her head leaves my chest. "You know how much crime happens in Phoenix every year?"

"That's different. We aren't talking about averages."

"What are we talking about?"

"Intent. We're talking about bad things happening to people who take all the precautions. In the city, crime happens to people who aren't ready. If you know what places to avoid and when not to go out you'll be fine. It isn't like that here. Things can happen no matter what you do."

"But I was alone. Doesn't that factor in with the chances?"

"I'm glad you feel safer with me around, but this is serious."

She pulls away from me. I hold her at arm's length. "I *am* safer with you around," she says, like I've insulted her. I have. I've insulted her choice in men. "I go all stiff, catatonic, when I'm scared. Once, a dog chewed my arm up and I couldn't even scream. It was like one of those nightmares. I'd probably let someone put a gun right to my head and pull the trigger without raising any fuss at all."

"Don't say that."

"It's true. It's like those people who faint at the sight of blood. What do you think there are people like that for? What advantage does it give them to be like prey?"

"You freeze up because you think it's hopeless to fight."

"What if it *is* hopeless? What if fighting only makes things worse for people like me? That dog was just looking for something to chew on. What if I just made it angry by fighting it?" I pull her back in again. Her voice vibrates in my chest. "I know it's important for you to be back here, but I wonder where I am in this inner landscape of yours. I wonder what I look like to you," she says.

I try to put a face to her voice, but it's a blur or is someone else. I hold her out by the shoulders as if to look at her. "You're right here."

"But you've never seen me. You don't know me like you do this place."

"No," I say, shaking my head. "But..." then I pass my hand through the Victrola that isn't there.

Night never comes. It's bright as day all the time and there's no looking away or covering the eyes. It helps to imagine the quiet light of the moon. The stars and the clouds lit improbably by it and the wind sweeping over fields of grass and the indiscernible distance of it all. But these things are not what carry over to the dream and I dream instead of the past, and of revelation only to wake without it. I strain to remember what it was but never can, because there was no revelation. It was an illusion.

She stands in the dark through a window, her face like the moon behind clouds. She stands among the lakeweed under black water, or far away in the nighttime woods in a white gown where I have to squint to see her propped unnaturally in the trees by some means. Always indeterminable, behind, under, or buried shallowly. What's curious by day is more in dreams where such uncanny visions strike terror.

Jessica is first to rise. I climb from bed an hour or so later and find her cooking eggs in the kitchen. She asks if I want some and if we should get a fire going. It isn't very cold. "I never thought I'd say that," she says. "'Get a fire going.'"

I decline and get ready in the bathroom and put

on some jeans and a jacket and return to the kitchen where Jessica is now plating the eggs, the wooden spoon tapping on a porcelain plate. "I'm going out again," I say, and imagine her turning sharply to look at me, arms crossed, spoon in her right hand. Faceless.

"Okay," she says, closer than I thought she was.

"I'll be back soon," I tell her, and move to her for an embrace but she's not standing there anymore. She'd gone back to the stove. "You know I don't like that."

"Don't like what?"

"You're moving like that on purpose." I feel for my boots by the door and slide them on then put Moxie into her harness. "I won't be gone long, alright?"

"Are you sure?"

"Yes. I'm just going to places I know."

"Places you knew, but things have changed, like you said. What if they've changed too much?"

"I won't get lost."

"At least tell me where you're going."

"South, to the tackle shop. I want to visit the owners if they're still alive."

"Can't I come with you?"

"I'd rather go alone," I say. A silence draws out. I can't even hear her breathing, can't envision her ghost standing there by the stove anymore. "Jessica?"

"I'm here," she says.

"Will you be alright?"

"Of course. I'll see you later," she says, then is silent again – is gone again – and I leave.

The sharp cold elicits visions of light through the trees

and little trinkets of ice in the grass. There were still patches of snow on the ground very late that spring. Nineteen-ninety-four, I believe.

There's smoke from a nearby chimney fire in the still morning air. It's quiet. No motorboats on the water this early, no traffic on the roads close enough to hush the little sounds of the waking woods. A squirrel scratches down the bark of a birch tree in bursts of movement, and birds call out in shy little chirps.

Moxie and I climb the grassy hill and onto the dirt path. Perhaps it's the case that I was born with the irony of photographic memory, or maybe it's the result of having only a few years' worth of imagery to draw from. But I'm certain I can navigate by feel the span of twenty miles around Burntside and to the Promontory on Little Bass Lake. I've returned to test if that's true, anyway. But much has changed, and lacking the benefit of knowing what at a distance, I must retrace my steps.

The sun is warm and the shadows are cold. From somewhere in memory I bring the woods in the dawn and the sight of our old neighbor coming out from the black-wooded cabin, hauling fishing gear down the steep fringe to his dock. From when? By the emotional charge of it, I should have been about ten years old. Definitely before everything, or such a morning would not have struck me at all, when there was always a sense of urgency and of keeping ahead of an idle mind.

We go left onto the dirt road, birch in rows upon rows along it, their pale stems against the fall-turned leaves. I go to them and reach out to touch the stem of the nearest. It's there, but the texture of the bark in memory is very different from what I feel. It isn't that it has simply grown, it's that my mind seems to take liberties with the details. And isn't it the details that make all the difference? Get the color of a man's eyes wrong and it's a different man.

We go on. In a half-mile we come to a forwarder sunken in the clay. Its axle had cracked in two long before I was born, and it was left here to decompose into dust. Counting the step from the trail I find it with the tires gone and the chassis brittle with rust. Deeper into the woods, there was a fire lookout tower. I take Moxie a short distance toward it but there's now a chain link fence blocking the way. Twigs twisted up in the wireworks. Minute currents of wind plucking and rattling the extent of it without pause. Moxie whines. We turn back.

The path is muddy with yesterday's rain. A blackbird calls, and there's an answer far away, then another one farther, and so on as some number of them pass the news of us on the path, southbound. Eventually the dirt path merges onto a paved road. A car whispers past us. There were no paved roads to Tucker's Tackle before. In a furlong or so, the road ends at a parking lot. A shopping cart rolls over the asphalt, heavy with groceries. Behind it is the clip of heels. Moxie does most of the navigating here, and she pulls right upon some indication of a crossing onto corrugated concrete. A sliding door opens and out comes another shopping cart with a toddler seated in the nest of it stuttering over words. My cane hits a metal bollard. A pair of them guarding the entrance from bad drivers. Through the doors is... unfamiliarity. Indescribable, except to say that reading of a place and hearing of it are comparable in limitation. Tucker's Tackle had been a converted home with a row of six parking spots and hardly more than two occupied at any time. Now, there's a parking lot to fit many more. I figured the exodus north of Burntside would have resulted in fewer people, but it seems the population has only shifted a little, closer to Ely proper.

Moxie puts her weight against the leash. She wants to go inside to a familiar environment, but I hold. From the sound of it the place has tripled in size. A young cashier greets customers and rapidly runs items over the scanner. No concord. The light returns, the static and waves of atoms, the halo.

Nothing for me here.

A mile more and the road leads to the fuel dock about the southern end of Burntside. The station sits at the mouth of a thread-thin river that winds five miles to Wolf Lake. I'd come here in a little red fishing boat our neighbor would lend me. I never paid for the fuel, but would simply pluck unguarded canisters from the dock and move on. I was old enough to understand it was theft, but by that time I knew what was in store for me and felt entitled to it. Entitled to everything, and figured I'd earned the right to help entropy along.

Near the water there's a radio on. Brittle voices go back and forth and over one another about prices slashed, percentages off, zero money down, yes. Zero. Money. Down. A lure plunges into the water and the fisherman ratchets up the line some. Then a speedboat comes cannonading the shoreline with some bass-heavy EDM track. I go on, and the radio fades behind a dozen or so boats chopping at the waves, going to and from the fuel docks, a cross-fire of competing music from every one of them and from the docks themselves. It's entirely too busy for this place to be a simple fuel station anymore.

Moxie takes us down a path off the road and over another parking lot and to the propped-open door and we go inside. There's a strong bilge odor combined with fresh plastics and mercaptan. An older man speaks to someone about optional insurance. The customer declines and the man steps away from the counter and plucks a set of keys from the pegboard wall, the little red floats tapping against each other. He gives the keys over and leads the customer to the door out to the docks. Engines idle in the water. Smell of gas.

He returns and greets me with a broad Tennessean accent. "What can I do for you?"

"I'm here to try my hand," I tell him.

The man grunts. "That dog trained to bark the location of another boat, or the make of a shoreline, I'd say whatever she's doin' for work now is a waste of talent."

"This isn't the old fuel dock I remember."

"No sir. We rent boats now."

"We? Are you the guy?"

I think he shakes his head. "My name's Henry," he says. "Though Tuckers' is plural, I ain't one of the brothers. Only the youngest of em's alive and he's in Minneapolis now." He'd been speaking down at some task on the counter top but the last he spoke directly at me. "Something familiar about you. Did you move into that little green cabin north of here?"

"That's the one."

He taps the countertop. "I thought it was a vulture swung in to lowball my poor friend." And he laughs. "But she wanted out before sellin' a home around here was impossible. Frightful old woman. I don't imagine she mentioned why?"

"She did. Bless her."

"You aren't worried about it, then? It's always young campers or hikers who go missing." What he's really saying is he thinks it's crazy for a blind man to wander around the wilderness with people going missing. "Some think it's the same person doing the killing now as all those years ago. But I don't think so. I think it's a copycat. That's what they call them."

Out the rear door an engine barks to life and the boat swings out on the deep water. Someone enters through the same door and the phone rings behind the counter. They answer it. The old man goes on, lowering his voice: "I think it's someone tryin' to tell a story with his crimes. A self-righteous kind of person. Someone eager to get caught, in a way, so they can talk about it and attract the makin' of a documentary about themselves. I bet they'd even take credit for those murders decades ago."

"I hope you're right," I say. "Any man not half-wanting to get caught never is. That's what I've come to know."

"Police haven't got a clue when the killer don't

paint a portrait of themselves all over the crime scene."

"Nobody knows it."

"Nobody damn well does, sir. So you ain't worried?"

"I've got my companion here. What about you?"

I'm sure that he shakes his head when he says, "Sixty-two years is a long time to see death coming. The prospect of it ain't new to me."

The other clerk says he has someone on the phone for the old man. We exchange goodbyes and I leave the way I came; past the brittle voices on the radio; past the grocery store and some miles past the watch tower that could be there or could not. It won't do to wander the places people are. I have to go north, where there's no one to have changed anything.

Aaron

Sergeant Gibbs runs a hand over his holster, the gun, his badge and his flashlight for some assurance they haven't leaped from his person in the last thirty seconds. Then he says, "You think we should pass a complaint for something?"

"For what?"

He can't seem to find comfort in his seat, or in his clothes, and he shifts and readjusts without pause. There's a soft ratcheting from his belt struggling to contain the weight he's gained. I feel I've done him a disservice by relegating him to the desk. "Wasting our time. My time," he says.

"You don't own your time. Plus, it's not like it was a false report, either."

"What about littering?"

"Did he litter?"

"Sure, that's how SAR found him. Left a trail of beer cans and bottles from... you know that old tower?"

I nod.

"There to Slim Lake."

"Then write up a charge and let his parents know."

"His fosters?" Gibbs reconsiders with a tilted wag of his head wag, eyes to the side. "They don't look the type to care, Chief."

"How so?"

His lips go into a puckered frown. "It's just, the mother cries, blames herself when I talk about her son."

"Ah, and I suppose threatening the kid with a criminal history won't do either."

"You know it. It's a game to him. A game to them too. We're tools for some manipulation between them."

"We do what we have to, Sergeant."

The man is now looking for something on my desk he's sure was there but isn't anymore. Then he looks out the glass door and down the long aisle of desks to a set of double doors which have just been disturbed, swinging back and forth on their hinges. "Here they are," he says, laments. The foster parents are making their way to Gibbs' desk now, led by our receptionist in her Tuesday dress. Blue. Battenberg lace. She motions for them to take a seat and they sit next to their sulking adopted son. "Do you want to charge him?" I ask.

He shakes his head. "Won't do any good. Can't really prove it was him anyhow. We'll just have to be there when he really screws the pooch. I'll tell him that, I think." The large man slaps his legs and stands, motions a weary goodbye and leaves my office. I watch him go to his desk and sit, a different person than the one a moment ago.

It's a glass office, mine. The front wall is divided by four parallel windows reaching floor to ceiling. The door is the kind at barber shops or convenience stores, and on it are vinyl letters as impermanent as those very businesses in the kiosks of strip malls. They display my name and title, but there's another man's name still fading from the glass. From my desk I've got a view of the entire floor. Men and women at work, or putting on the act. I've been Chief of Ely City Police for eight months. The name still fading is Cass Philbrook. He'd been Chief for twenty-six years until resigning after murders began popping up in the area again. One day he tells me of a nightmare he had where he'd stared into the workings of a grandfather clock and saw a black cat peering back at him through the glass, lounging strangely within the gearworks behind the pendulum. He took some private meaning from it and laid out on this desk the tools of his traffic: revolver, badge, a leather bandolier. Then the man left without another word. He passed a month later from an overdose on pain pills, and I guess that makes for one way out. As for me, there are three: the front door, then the side door that goes into Webb's office, and last, the window that I could make an exit of if it came to it. Two stories down are the pallid tops of police cruisers to cushion a fall.

By Gibbs' desk, the foster father begins his lecture. His hand shakes and his forefinger is arced like a worn coat hanger. I see what Gibbs meant. It's in the father's eyes that he has no real hope of getting through to his son. It's the performance of lecturing. There's no anger at all. Dim eyes on a dim face. This is the second time in two months the young man has been lost and found again. People go missing all the time in Ely. Most are found strung out in one of the city's infarcted limbs. Now and then someone is found dead – killed by the elements or by somebody. The kid wears a shirt too small for him and pale jeans and dirty white sneakers. Something about him looks the part of a body you'd find, ill-dressed against the wilderness and too young to know it doesn't reciprocate fondness.

Webb raps on the side door and comes through before I can answer. "Aaron," he says.

"Sean."

He stands near my desk and looks out the glass door to the ensuing lecture and folds his arms. "You think we should threaten charges?"

"Gibbs suggested the same. Then he said it won't work, and I agree. The kid'll be drunk-lost again in a month or so. We've nailed down his pattern at least."

Captain Webb breathes. He's got his black binder with him, rapping his forefinger and middle against it. Tap tap, tap. It's something important he wants to discuss, in the binder. Something he disagrees with me on, by is reluctant to start to get around to. "Guy shot last night on second street and Boundary wasn't armed," he says. "Didn't even threaten the defender with harm, according to both of them."

"That's a shame. He admitted to that?"

"He sure did. But I don't care, personally. Do you?"

"Not really. Intent bears the means."

"What's that?" he asks, sensing they aren't my words.

"Some judge I read said it. Muggers are typically armed, so it's reasonable to assume."

He nods. "Anyway, I'll interview our defender today or tomorrow when he's calmed down."

"Just don't get him to say anything really stupid."

"It's not up to me. He talks into the silence like a guilty man. Talks and talks."

"Do you want me to do it?"

"I got it."

Sean lets a silence sink in. I suppose he's waiting for permission. "If there's more, then let's have it," I say.

He moves to my desk and pushes aside the nameplate at the center of it and slaps down his binder like I'm some interview of his, then he sits and says, "The man went missing from campsite fifteen eighty-nine? Won't be found within ten miles of it."

"You offer it up like a wager."

"If you've got money to lose."

"The man's on foot and missing for thirty-six hours. Experienced hiker. We'll find him within one." Sean shakes his head like he knows something. His uncouth mannerisms make him look like an adolescent at times. He is young. Thirty-something. Probably last a good ten years before he's driven to search and rescue or some other non-C.I.D with better endings. "Well?" I say.

He whips open his binder scrawled with shorthand, and pinned to the pages are some evidentiary photographs. The binder is his physical connection to the work. He says it's easier to remember details by writing them down, by "handling" them. Something about the smell of the pages and the scratch of a pen to make a fanfare of it; make cross-referential details for easy recall. "The body six months ago was found here –" he points to a map of Fenske Lake – "he was reported missing outside Winton and his gear was found not far from where he'd last been seen. Like he was forced to ditch it and taken by gunpoint."

"His is already declared homicide. Other than a general location, what pattern can be had from a single body?"

"Six bodies, sir," he says.

I could have guessed. It's that desire to connect everything in one unifying theory. Only, I know otherwise. "What has you reaching back so far?"

He's got a section on the map bracketed in red pen. It's a thirty-square-mile area north of Ely, encompassing all locations where a body has turned up in the last twenty-five years. He's wrong if he thinks it's the same person responsible for all of them. The land north of Burntside is tens of miles of abandoned rural pathology. Most likely, it's some mutt squatting in an abandoned structure opportunistically picking off lone wanderers.

"I've bracketed a search around campsite fifteen-eighty-nine," I tell him. "But, if we find nothing, we'll send the hounds for a body wherever you think we'll find one, Captain."

"A body can wait till then," he says, folding the binder, standing and leaving out the side door.

The lecture seems to be over. The kid at Gibbs' desk has seen me peering out at him through the narrow window, and it's occurred to him he's a spectacle. The subject of scorn. Look around, kid. Don't you know what they do here? They've little chance and you're no help at all. Least you could do is look embarrassed but you've no tact either.

Now I want to charge him with something. But why bother? Punishment marks the ego with the faux pas, at his age. Perhaps at any. He'd only lean into delinquency afterwards.

They stand from the desk and make a slow exit, aware they are the actors here. The adoptive father, taken by his cameo role, has a final word with his adopted son before the double doors close.

William

The day following Jessica rises before her alarm. Her bare feet tap over the hardwood into the enjoined bathroom. She turns the faucet and it sputters into the sink, the iron-rich water wafting hints of the containment into the air like from blood in the lungs.

She lets it run for a time while the brown water turns clear and then she starts to brush her teeth. I don't stir. When finished, she lets Moxie out of the crate and goes to the kitchen and sets the percolator onto the stove. Her phone chimes the time and she comes in and turns it off. Still, I don't stir. Moxie's claws scratch over the hardwood as she follows her about and to the driftwood table where Jessica sits and drags her canvas purse over the top of it, searching through it. The dull chimes of keys held against resonance in her hand. The coffee begins to roll and pop on the stove and she takes it off the heat and pours it into a vessel and twists the top on. She says something to Moxie then leaves out the door.

Why did pretend to be asleep? Reluctant, perhaps, to tell her where I was going, but of course, that's no good reason at all.

Tally it against sleep with the others. What's another five minutes of rumination each night?

I get up and ready for the day. The water from the tap still tastes of iron. Moxie waits at the door and I put her into the harness and grab the backpack of supplies. Inside is a pouch with water and some protein bars; a flashlight to alert others; a knife and a ferrocerium rod with a ball of cotton kindling. I take up the white cane and leave out the door. It's seven-thirty and thirty-three degrees. The snow has long since melted but it's still too cold for mosquitoes. They'll be out in clouds in a month or so.

We go north up Hanson Road past some new homes, these evidenced by paved driveways and big gates that tremble in the wind. I count four such driveways before the tracks in the mud become too narrow to be passenger cars. Probably ATV's and dirt-bikes. We come to a trail veering north-west and follow it. It's not long when it splits. Right will take us to Ember Stone. A popular spot for little weddings above Burntside, or so it was until the jut of rock slid into the lake after two weeks of rainfall. Moxie and I turn left, which goes a couple miles to Fox Elementary School. Never learned the address. Never needed to, and neither did I follow the roads or trials to school as a kid, but I'm not confident enough to cut through the woods, so we keep to well-trodden ground.

Starlings have taken roost in the trees on either side of the trail and they call to each other without pause. Leaves pat down softly onto the duff all around us. None of it corroborates a specific memory. It could be any place there are starlings to sing and leaves to fall. The wynd itself has no distinctive features either, yet I hold it all so clearly in imagination. I can only guess how this is possible, but if I had to, I'd compare it to recognizing a person by the way they breathe. Perhaps you can do the same with a location by the way the wind blows? There are other clues too, such as the engines on the water miles away, chortling just above idle tempo, then sprinting from their docks one by one and bounding over waves, each with their own direction.

There's a fallen aspen lying across the trail. The stem is two feet in diameter and the wood is light and frays apart easily, like coarse hair tightly bound. Parts of it are trampled to splinters by foot traffic and by vehicles. I go on.

One of the boats sound like it's coming in close to the shore. It isn't a boat at all, but a diesel truck by the sound. It comes close enough to quiet the birds around me. And what sound like empty propane tanks are tumbling around in the bed of the pickup. Moxie brings us off the trail and we wait together as it nears, the tanks rattling violently. I collapse the white cane and hold it at my sides. They're definitely in a hurry. Fifteen an hour at least on the narrow trail meant only for foot traffic. It bounces past but does not continue on, but stops abruptly, sending the tanks slamming into the back of the cab. The suddenness of it speaks of confrontation. Perhaps I've trespassed? Moxie puts her body across my leg. "Good morning," I say. There's no reply but the idle engine. "Are you lost?" I try. The passenger window slides down and from the cab a radio broadcast gives the weather for the day. Nothing from the driver. The timing is wrong, the cadence of normal interaction, wrong. With that I start down the path again, and after a time the truck continues on also. When it's far enough away I take Moxie off the path and into the woods to avoid roads and pathways for the remainder of the hike.

Moxie whines. She doesn't want to go off the trail, but after that, I don't think it's a good idea to stay on them. "I know the way, girl. Just don't let me hit my head on anything, alright?" I say, extending the white cane ahead of me. We trod on. In the woods, with its many features, the remembering comes slow. But each step necessitates the recollection of the next. A confluence of senses, feel, sound and even smell, work like coordinates onto a time and place. I step as I would have those years ago, some calisthenic calculus turning out predictions – place my hand here, foot there, turn such a way and the noise from the speedboats far away struck my ears just so. Moxie is keen on a direction and I oblige, if only to test the limits of this. We go blind some distance into the woods and I lose place many times. The going is slow and meticulous, swinging the cane out, tamping the ground ahead with one foot before committing with the next. But then I have it again: where I am, exactly, and I can pad easily from place to place like a line was drawn from one remembered thing to the next. But as fast it comes, it's gone. I lose frame. Lost it a few paces ago actually. Discord. I've grown and it's not possible to go as I did before. It might also be that I never went this particular way, or that I'm traveling the inversion of my usual path through this part of the woods – from school back home where I was more inclined to take shortcuts. I was so sure a moment ago! I must have imagined it. False remembrance, and if here, where else? What else?

We begin again. A strange quiet has developed all around us. No birds. We are all that moves now, that makes a sound. Then, Moxie stops and pulls against my efforts to urge her on. It's now that I wonder what got her interest in the first place? She's trained to ignore distractions, but that relies on being in a place similar to where she had been trained. I really have turned her into a pet. When I moved here I was advised to pair with another dog, but I argued it would be troublesome to train and bond with a new one. What nonsense.

I tug on the leash and give the usual commands but Moxie remains immovable, and she's lost to the mind as prey hiding in the brush is lost to the eye. It dawns on me then that I'm oblivious to some danger, to something that watches me, and I go still for better listening. The boats far away have gone silent having reached their destinations', but still I hear nothing, and neither does Moxie make a sound.

It's something she caught the scent of back there. Something on the ground at the end of her snout. I kneel and pat her head then feel for her muzzle. Shallow, rapid breaths. Out of order: in in, in again, exhale, exhale again. She won't pull away, as if she's guarding food. I reach out and touch whatever it is she is so interested in – cold and calloused. My body knows before my mind does. I pull away by instinct. It's a human foot. It's a body.

I stand and speak into the silence. Something apologetic, like I've just stumbled on a sleeping man. There's no reply. "Are you alright?" I say. No hope of a response. I know it already. They're dead and can't answer and I'm just standing here! Something moves before I do. Fast through the leaves. A rapid patter of paws raking out earth as they approach, weaving between the trees. Moxie intercepts the rushing animal and a violent struggle ensues. Teeth and torsioned muscle. She's lost in the sound of it all. I pull at the harness to separate them and kick benignly at the assaulting animal but it's useless. I feel on the ground for a stone or anything to use and come up with just twigs and dirt and pebbles. Above the fight are voices of men coming closer, rushing in. Moxie shrieks. She's losing. The other is made for fighting – but Moxie fights on. She's a shepherd. Nothing gets the better of her unscathed. She's got something of the attacker in her jaws and she's wrenching her body back and forth until it tears from the attacker's skull and hot blood lashes out in strands and in loops. The attacking dog lets out its own shriek which turns at once into one of ferocity and it fights with new tenacity. Something else tears. It's Moxie's nape. She yelps for mercy and submission. The fight is gone from her and she lies down on the ground now, but submission is not what the other is after, and it goes on wrenching her neck back and forth. I roll on top of the animal and use the weight of my body to crumple it under me, then I snake my arm under its throat and use everything I have to close it up, the esophagus and the arteries. At last it sees that I'm a threat and lets go of Moxie and pulls its body under me with explosive bursts of its legs. With its short and stout neck and small skull the thing is able to slide free from under my arms. Moxie attacks again, regaining its aggression.

The voices are close now. Words edge out over the fray. "Ban's got him over here!" says a man bounding to us. I undo the harness and get to my feet. I'm sorry... I must run, and I turn and dash into the woods, into the shapeless light. Low hanging branches lash my face and I bring up my arms to shield it. Everything is forgotten in the panic, and a heedless step takes me over a ledge and I tumble down with shrill discomfort in my guts, rolling and skidding a ways until landing in a knot of woody talons. I scramble through them, opening abrasions between my fingers. The stems are hard and they come straight up from the ground like grass. The leaves on the stems are few or absent. It's red osier.

Suddenly, there's the sharp crack of a rifle shot. Close enough to be the target. It rebounds off the facets of the land, each echo weaker than the last, and they expire at an undetermined point, the sound of it brought again to the mind with as much certainty as the final echo. No pain. It was for Moxie.

I crawl through the dogwood and when clear of it, stand and run headlong through the woods. A bright forest. Blinding phantasmagoria like the flora of stars. I glance my shoulder off the stem of an ash tree. There's something about the shape of it and of its roots loping up from the earth. I rush on, over a scattering of boulders where rills run between. The placement of them... and then I have it: still frames slide into place; the ground; the trees farther and farther away and then the school. I go through an extent of old brambles hanging down all around. My boots spare me from twisting my ankles many times, and again when I stumble over a pile of dead tree limbs. I crawl over them, then stand and go on. New channels have been carved out from years of rain. The ground has changed. Losing it. Lost. Running blind again.

This is foolish! I can't outrun them, but I know this place better than they do. I can use that.

The ground flattens out over a field of bluestem. It must the elementary school. A playground should lie just ahead. Swing sets and a blue castle with slides and orange awning on the highest tower. I go and find it there, the metal supports rusted and the plastic sagged. I duck through it, hands probing the way ahead. A flock of birds have made roost here and they take flight, their wings fanning the stench of avian stagnation into the air. Loose feathers drifting down as they go up, squawking my location to the men in pursuit.

The main school building lies ahead. A single-story longhouse with cinder block walls and thin clerestory windows above eye-level. The gym is east. Gray fox mascot emblazoned on its southern wall. I go there and find the double doors gone. Window glass on the black mastic floor. Something in the side office is startled when I enter, casting plastic chairs aside and its hooves clipping frantically over the grimy linoleum right past me, having no other place to go. Should I turn back? Back where?

The torn floors in the hall crack under my feet as I trace the length of the cinder-block wall and enter the basketball courts. There, a blank. Think! Games of parachute, dodgeball, basketball... me taking no part and sat in a corner fiddling with my shoelaces. Is that all? No. I'd slip into the locker rooms when the PE coach wasn't paying attention and hide there in one of the stalls. Follow. Piles of cardboard, wood, trash on the courts, hopeless to avoid. In the locker room, the sound of my boots bounce off the tile walls. A nest of hatchlings in one of the sinks all fall silent, go still, and from somewhere I pull the sight of their trembling heads tracking me with large onyx marble eyes as I go past. There's a subtle current of air from a door cracked slightly open. I shoulder through to the outside where another series of frames slide into place: a field of grass to a berm of trees; a twisting path all of my own making to a small den made by foxes under the roots of oak trees. The field is exposed but there is no time to find another way. I step out, silent as I can manage, listening for movement in the surrounding woods. The wind picks up, howling in my ears. I reach the berm and push through the thick bundle of dry branches that shatter like ancient bones. Ahead are the dens dug out beneath the roots. A place where no one could find me. But I'm grown now. It's not possible to go through them as I did before, so I step over them. The old roots snap under me, and under them is a deep recess. A place perhaps large enough for me to hide, lie low, and I do. A foul den recently occupied. The ribs of rodents everywhere like discarded hair clips.

Be still. They're out in the field now, gliding through the bluestem. Three men and the dog whimpering with pain and desperate hunger. All stop in the middle of the clearing. Voices. One of them says, "Shut him up."

"He's hurt!" says another. "We need to go back!"

"No, we're on him. Look." They fall silent. Can they see me?

"Are we tracking him or tracking that?" says a third man. There's a crash in the brush some thirty yards behind me. Something like a deer bounds away.

The first who spoke says, "he saw you?"

"He was on the road in. I didn't think he'd turn off it. His mutt must've picked up the scent of the dead," says the second man, younger than the other two.

"We give Ban his, and we'll find him before sundown," says the third. The dog, Ban, lashes against its leash. It has my scent already. The thing is growling right at me. My heart is thundering in my ears and it's hard to hear what they're saying. They're certainly whispering to one another like they've realized I'm close. But then, they leave.

Still, I won't move Even to breathe grates the roots against one another, and I fear to do even that. A keen ear will hear it. But it's only a whisper, hardly perceptible even to my own ears! The birds are returning, circling above, swooping down in a murmuration to roost in the old jungle gym again. The men must be gone after all, so I crawl, the weight of my body never placed entirely onto one or even two arms or to the shines or knees. I press through the ropy tangles and the knots of gnarled roots, break through thick spider webs with colonies of them scattering over my arms and face, pushing through the damp earth, bit and stung, but the pain of it is put far away somewhere. Further than the pain is an elision of all visual memory. I project myself through it: the school and the camp and the long trek to her house and farther.

Something moves near, closer. One of them must have stayed behind, and now he's heard me and comes to investigate. I go still, and hope that I've become indistinguishable from the roots and buckthorn with all the mud caked onto my clothes. An ant colony is enraged by my presence, but they can have the hand swarmed with them now. I won't move. Certainly not from pain, but neither when the wind picks up to obscure the sounds of things, daring me to use the moment for escape.

<u>Aaron</u>

When the call comes in it's played for laughs and for bets. "What's a blind man doin' in the middle of the woods?" demands Gibbs. The group clustered in the cubicles nearest him jeer.

"Your kind of job, seeing that you'll find him within thirty yards of his front door," says Jefferson at his desk.

Gibbs spins in his chair and slaps the rests as he stands. It's like he has to make noise any way he can. Tapping the tops of desks, slamming doors loudly, so on. He checks his belt and radio and snatches his cap from the top of his desk.

"I won't need help," I tell him.

He looks at me. "What, you're going?"

"I can't stand it here after a while," I say. "Besides, you look busy."

"You sure? I complain but it's just noise. I don't mind going."

"I don't mind either." I scratch at my five-days beard, flakes of dandruff on my shirt.

"When's the last you've seen yourself? All do respect," he says.

He's right, so I shave and take a hot sink bath in the restroom and step into a clean set of plain clothes I keep in my office for just such occasions. Black fired denim pants and a journeyman with a place for the badge. I look myself over in the foggy mirror, itself reflected by smaller mirror behind me above a pot of devil's ivy on a desk. Christ, I look tired. But I don't *feel* tired. The badge, yes, the badge: I pin it to the jacket and it hangs there, top heavy, like some worn symbol of a long-extinct orthodoxy.

Averaging fifteen over the speed limit I'm there in twenty minutes. I turn down the grassy driveway, amber light from the windows of the cabin winking in and out between the trees like eyes spying my approach. A pale face in the kitchen window broods over the sink in the kitchen. The woman looks up when she spots my headlights. Must be the one who called it in: Jessica Albane, if I recall right. She disappears momentarily then opens the door before I even stop the car on the top of the hill. I call my arrival in through the radio and the girl has her arms folded, making herself small. I step out. She looks me over, my jeans and jacket and badge, and it's clear that she expected the cavalry and is dismayed to have received some house-mouse instead. "Ms. Albane?"

A brief smile that doesn't reach her eyes. "Yes, hello," she says. Her face is wider than it is tall, or it looks that way with the bangs to her brow. She's small and neotenous and I wonder what she's thinking, entrusting herself to a blind man.

"Aaron McLloyd," I say. She doesn't want to be touched. Her hands are squeezed pale between the crooks of her arms, so I just nod the initiative. "You called about your missing fiance?"

"Yes, come in."

The door opens up to the kitchen. On the stove dinner is cooked and cooled to room temperature again. Four fillets of walleye. One of them has been nibbled on. We sit opposite each other near the fireplace in the living room. The place smells of moving boxes. I pull out a notepad and unsheathe a pen from the spiraled wire. The notepad serves to signal a start to our business, and the girl tucks herself into her seat and seems to prepare.

"You say William has been gone for..."

"Four hours, when I called it in," she says. "Six hours as of now... I know it's not a long time but –"

"Never mind apologies. Did he tell you where he was going?"

"He messaged me at nine. Said he was going north, up the road to Echo Trail."

I scrawl it down. "You say he's blind? How blind are we talking here?"

"Totally."

"And he's got a guide-dog with him?"

"Yes, Moxie. She's trained for the city, so there's a chance –" She stops short, ceding to the sound of my pen lashing the pages of the notepad.

"A chance that what?"

"That Moxie got them lost."

"What kind of dog is Moxie?"

"A German Shepherd. Girl."

"What's William wearing?"

"I wasn't there when he left this morning." I look

up at her. "But, probably his usual: Brown boots. Dark pants. Jeans. A shirt and jacket."

"What kind of boots"

"I'm not sure."

"What size?"

"Twelves, I think." She holds herself and shakes her head. "God, why don't I know these things?"

"Any gear for camping? For survival?"

"He has a backpack with some rations in it. Maybe a day's worth."

"Anything for shelter? Any weapons?"

"I don't think so." The girl breathes.

She thinks I'm running a script. I am of course. "Just getting a sense for urgency," I tell her, and her eyes go down to her feet. She wants something to do with her hands but there's nothing to do so she hooks her thumbs in the loops of a crochet blanket over her lap. I sheath the pen and say, "with few supplies, and his condition, our search bracket is probably small. It's hard to think he's traveled far from Echo Trail even if he meant to."

"He knows this place. He used to live here when he had his sight," she says.

"He lived in the area?"

"In this cabin, in fact."

I figured it already. Came here to be sure and now I'm looking over the room for anything that might say without a doubt. The Compton place has changed hands a couple times. There are no mementos left from them that I can see in the living room. "What places does he know?" I ask.

"He mentioned his elementary school, a camp. He can recall things almost perfectly. That's what he says. We came here because it's easier for him." She shakes her head, unable to keep some sense of irony finding expression. I stand. "Wait, is that all? Are we done?" she asks.

"Done for now," I say. She stands too. "We'll use scent dogs to find him. Anything he's worn will do."

"I'll get something." She leaves to the bedroom on the right of the brick fireplace and returns with a white hamper-crumpled undershirt and holds it out for me. I unfold a plastic bag from an inseam pocket of my jacket and hold the mouth of the bag open. "Does it matter that I've touched it?" she asks. I shake my head and she drops it in and I seal the bag shut and tuck it under my arm. I'm searching the room again... for something. "Is there anything more you need?"

"No, nothing more."

"When will you begin?"

"Immediately. I doubt he'll give us much of a chase," I say, and try for a smile, but it falters and she sees. "We'll let you know as soon as we find him," I add, then leave out the door and hurry back to my jeep.

In the darkening woods the gaps between the trees or the trees themselves take the forms of men. Their faces are anonymous, cold, looking on unblinkingly. A good man is well-advised to perform for such illusory audiences. Even godless men who say strange things to themselves such as 'karma' or that all deeds are recorded in light where an instrument will one day play the whole of our history back to alien observers. Under such notions immoral men can hold themselves to moral standards.

In the Jeep I call dispatch for backup and for canine units and direct them all to Echo Trail, then fire up the engine and whip it around to meet them there.

William

Hours have gone. Crickets chirp in the dark and a nightjar trills softly with them. When the man in the field moves they all fall silent, and he goes still and won't move until they start up again. It's this, back and forth until he steps into the thicket of buckthorn I'm hiding in. The man himself is not heard, only what he disturbs, and even then there's hardly any sound at all. Maybe there's no one? Maybe I've imagined the presence of something creeping around in the dark?

A confluence of quiet, the night critters and the wind coming to a common pause before all go on again, the wind and the crickets and the nightjar; and the man nears. I fear to breathe, but the need to becomes urgent and I'm feint from the effort to keep from breathing. There's no resisting it for long, and I take air into my lungs and my chest presses out against the woody talons to produce reticulation through the roots. I can hear it in my bones. Does he?

He comes in closer – very near now. No choice but to act, and soon, so I circuit my hand to the rear-most pocket of my backpack and pinch the zipper tab and pull it open. Quiet, but distinct from the sounds of the wilderness around us. The man goes still when he hears it, and so do I. The both of us move only when the other does. I manage to get the flashlight in my hand. The weight of the man presses down on the roots, but still I don't hear him breathing at all! He stops. Something keeps him from going on. He must know I'm close. Right under him!

Heart beating in my throat, behind my eyes. A phantom pain spreads over my back in anticipation of being shot here in the mud, but nothing comes. Never a sound from the hunter. Everything is still. Everything watches.

Movement again, the tangled buckthorn curls over me and the shank of a boot steps down onto my right arm. It was unintentional, but he must feel the presence of something beneath, some fleshy thing, because he stops and does not put all his weight down through the boot, but probes the unmistakable make of an arm with it. It must be now!

I ram my shoulder into the back of his knees. He yelps with surprise and falls into the roots and mud. I pull at his arms in search of whatever weapon he carries. There! A rifle. He's bear-hugging it and he begins shouting for help when I grab hold of it. There is no reply to his calls. I'm stronger than he is, but not so much that I can wrench the rifle easily from his grasp, so I get a knee up onto the man's chest and pull. He holds with a grip to tear the ligaments of his hands, but a finger comes away, then another and I twist the rifle free. I fall back and get to my feet and point the weapon in his direction. I've pulled the trigger already, but it didn't fire. Jammed, and now I'm fumbling for the action only to find nothing, so I just hold the barrel of it on him anyway. "Okay, okay!" he says. "I was just lost. I didn't mean to trespass."

"Stay there," I say, treading back. Stumbling. The flashlight isn't in my hands anymore and I've no idea where it could be. Movement. "I said stay."

"I'm not moving!" he pleads.

"Hands up. Way up. Above your head."

"They're up!"

I try for a lever but there isn't one. "Stand. Slow. Use only your legs."

"Okay," he says and it sounds like he grips the branch of the nearest tree to pull himself off the ground. "I was just... tracking a kill."

"You think I'm stupid? What were you hunting with a twenty-two?"

"I was..."

"You were the one in that truck back there, right? On the trail?"

He says nothing.

"Well, were you?"

"No," he says.

"What's your name?"

"My name?" he repeats. By the sound of it he's looking behind him.

"Look at me. Your name."

"Tanner," he says. I believe him. He's too slow to have pulled that one out of his ass. "What about the other two? What are their names?"

"There's no one else."

"Yes there is. The other two men with that dog, Ban, was it?"

"I don't know."

"You don't know? Keep your hands up."

"I haven't moved them!" he says. I need to get out of here.

"Alright Tanner, turn away. Keep those hands raised!"

"I won't let you shoot me in the back," he says.

"Do as I say, and I won't have to. Turn and go back the way you came in. All the way back."

"Can I have my rifle? I'll just go, I swear."

"Oh, sure thing," I tell him. "I'll give it back a piece at a time. The bullets first. Where do you want them? The heart? The head?"

"Alright, I'm going," he says, but doesn't go on. I'd have shot him then if I could. It'd be an easy thing for him to draw a pistol from his waist without me knowing it, and there's been more than enough time for him to do it.

"Go," I say, and listen close as he stumbles his way back through the tangle of buckthorn and the oak roots and onto the field. When he's far enough I sling the rifle over my shoulder and turn the opposite way and work quickly through the thick brush. There's no time to search for anything that might bring this place into focus, into mind, and for a while there's nothing but some latent familiarity about the area, like a scent you know but can't place. No visualizations come to me, but I have a sense for things like the ground and how to avoid the thickest patches of brush and trees. The bony branches pull open old abrasions and open new ones over my face and arms, but that doesn't matter. Movement somewhere. I stop and listen. Four-legged things at both my flanks. Coyotes perhaps, come to see what fumbles so noisily in the dark. They follow for a time and coo and clap their jaws then move on. After a while, I emerge from the dense brush and onto a slight acclivity. The ground is damp and hard. If I've placed myself square, I'll ascend a half-mile or so then down sharply onto the road that leads to the camp.

Slippery mud all the way up. Maybe an hour or so hiking when the ground turns flat. A brief gust of wind sweeps windrows of leaves past my feet and down the slope I climbed. Farther on, my boots crack over a slab of stone embedded solidly in the clay. By instinct or muscle memory, I pitch forward and plant my hands on the smoothed rock to scamper its vantage; body before mind again, and when my mind comes around I know that it's a particular boulder jutting out from the ground like a broken bone. Tectonic iconography scoring the middle of it. Three vertical fissures like bolts of lighting recorded in stone. The clay the boulder spurns is all that keeps it from splitting in half.

From a long time ago I hear my father telling me not to drag my feet. "You're just about all that's large enough to snap the twigs on the ground. You and bears and both are a danger to deer. They've learned to listen for it, understand?" He took up a stick from the ground and snapped it in half and then he marched around in the dead leaves with his feet high, stepping between the fallen twigs. "See? It's how they tell what's a danger to them and what isn't. Keep your feet high and watch your step. Move like they do," he said, and he waited for me to make eye contact as some indication I'd heard him.

We stalked through the forest for a couple hours. I'd seen wild animals only a handful of times before, but on that day the woods were alive with rabbits and foxes and deer, having carved a delicate path through their most fundamental defenses. We spotted a lone buck near the great boulder I stand now. My father told me to take the shot and I did; aim, steady, fire. The deer bounded away unfazed. "Missed," I said, but dad insisted that we go after him. I wanted to ask why but he put a finger to his mouth for quiet and we went to the boulder, and on the gray and black-speckled granite were drops of blood bright as poinsettia. "I got him?"

"Yes. In the flank. It's important we find him now. It's bad to wound an animal and let it get away. Let's see where it went from up there," he said.

We climbed the formation and scanned the forest for the buck and spotted it ambling as though unharmed over the terrain some distance away... yes, in that direction.

Witnessing it shrug off a gunshot wound appealed to a different part of me. "Won't it heal?" I asked my father.

"It's working off adrenaline. If it heals it'll be enfeebled for the rest of its life."

"Will anything help it along?"

"Help it how? It's grown. Nothing will look after it. It'll be eaten by bears or shot by other hunters very soon." He gave me a look, his eyes shrouded partly by the brim of his cap, and perhaps he saw something on my face and thought it was necessary to make an exception for me – his wounded son – and he said, "People live just fine with injuries, but an animal can't. They don't have our wits." The mood took on a self-conscious quality. He adjusted his cap low over his eyes and he scrunched his large sharp nose, his graying beard exaggerating the movements of his chin and upper lip. "Do you want to take it?" he asked. I spied the deer through the scope of my ruger; the picture obscured by entoptic apparitions like I'd stared too long at the sun and a green facsimile of it remained there at the center of my vision.

"I can't."

"It's okay." He brought the stock to his shoulder and with both eyes open, one through the scope and the other keeping view of our surroundings, he shot the buck through the heart. There's no ignoring a heartshot, and it leaped once into the air then came down like a bag of loose meat and bones. We went to the killed animal where its blood painted the lobes of bracken draped around it; eyes still full of life but there was none. My father knelt and dressed it in minutes, separating the organs that he put in a pile in the bushes. "Think you can carry it?" he asked.

I knelt and pulled the torso off the ground by the forelegs. "I think so."

From far away comes the choked cry from the hound in pursuit of me. I thought taking the rifle would have discouraged them from following, but they don't think like rational people do. It has my scent now. That's certain. There's blood around my collar from the cuts on my face and I think I've soiled my clothes, having no time at all to stop in the bushes. Everything aches, but there are no significant injuries and I've still got strength left in my legs. The problem isn't exhaustion, though. It's that I have no idea where to go from here.

After the kill, we'd gone back the way I just came from. No choice then. Have to push north, blind. Nothing for a while. The dog and the hunters are gaining ground as I sift through the possibilities before me. Nothing fits. Probably, the land has changed too much for recognition. As if in answer, my foot finds air where I thought ground would be, and I tumble headlong over a short drop and roll onto my back. No worse off, I stand and turn and pat with my hands the crescent-shaped ledge I fell down. It's a scar from a landslide. I continue on and find more of these, some larger and some smaller. Down and down again, then onto a mound of loose regolith, and from this onto solid ground. Heavy branches hang low and I duck under them. Three-lobed leaves, the edges serrated. It's maple. Means I'm presently on a ridge some thirty yards above the road that goes to camp. Saw them from the bus on the way there: hedgerow of maple on the butte along the road, broad and low to the ground like they'd developed under some barrier.

I start down carefully; little landslides with each step, the sediment tumbling on ahead and thwacking off the stems of more maple trees clinging to the scarp. I slide over exposed bedrock, then onto scree at the bottom. The road is overgrown with switchgrass. I ease at once into a jog. This is my chance to widen the distance between us. They've gained ground on me. The hungry cries of the dog are coming over the hills and over the stirring forest, and soon there are no hills between us, and the cries reach my ears directly from the ridge I stood maybe ten minutes ago. They're close enough to hear me on the macadam, so I take a knee and fumble over the rifle for its workings. It's a semiautomatic. There's a round jammed in the ejection port and I clear it by racking the charging handle several times. The clip release is behind the trigger, the safety at the front of the guard.

The hound chokes against its collar. Its claws scrape over the dirt and stone as it comes down with the men following in silence. I take aim, and... what if it's rescue? No, they would make themselves known.

Finger to the trigger.

What if they know people are hunting me? They would understand the danger and would not announce themselves. Suppose it's the police who have picked up my trail? *Suppose you sit here and let them advance on you?* I have to call out to them first. And, before further objections, I call into the dark. I'm not really sure what. I felt nothing of it in my own throat.

All else goes silent. The hound is culled, its cries and movements. Only the sleepwalking stir of the woods now. The croaking amphibians somewhere off the road, small creatures skittering in the fallen and wet leaves, an easterly wind through the trees. I fire. The shot snaps my hearing away for a time and, slowly, it returns to find only the wind, but even that expires. The moon! It's full this time of month. Can they see me? In answer, another shot rings out. The bullet shrieks high above me then shatters to pieces on a stone face somewhere, the lead core whistling its trajectory into a tree. Our intentions known to one another, I begin down the road again as quickly as I can. All is silent on the ridge. They move carefully now or not at all, while I run until my lungs are raw with the night air and my legs burn. The ghost-light pulsing in waves of atoms with the heart. I travel perhaps a mile, then come to a roofed sign on the verge of the road with my steps rebounding off its flat surface. I run my hand over the raised letters to be sure. I'm tall enough now to touch the asphalt shingles. They crumble at my fingertips.

Ahead, where the road ends, lies the Common Lodge of Slim Lake Camp. The two-story A-frame once greeted arrivals with a facade of dark wood and a pair of large angle-top windows glowing with amber light apt the promise of warmth and food.

Follow, to a dirt roundabout where the buses had gone to let everyone off. A corral. Ropes hung loosely between the stanchions, six on either side. Both are gone but I respect them anyway. Only, that's not right, is it? On the bus here, I helped instigate a desire for us all to run as soon as the doors opened. We stood from our seats and crowded the isle, and as soon as the bus came to a stop we broke from the confines of the greyhound like escaped prisoners. Over or under the ropes meant to corral us into lines, each with our own point of interest. A middle-aged woman had ridden with us, recording our misbehavior with pen and paper. She demanded that we settle ourselves down but we ignored her. Strength in numbers.

I darted between the stanchions toward the rifle range where the white and red targets stood out against the colors of the woods. But, I never made it. *Go back.*

Over my dash to the range a man's shouted that I wouldn't so much as catch the sight of a rifle if I took another step. He was wearing khakis and a white tee-shirt with the camp's logo, and it was just the right kind of threat, so I turned back at once and fell in line. The girl's from another bus made a parallel line and they'd been instructed to hold onto each others' backpacks like little ducklings. We were told to do the same but to hell with that, and to the recollection – it would have me turning back to the corral anyway.

We were led to the common lodge. The double doors are gone. Battered down by vandals or time. Inside it's quiet as an empty cellar. Abandonment felt in the way the wind filters through the doorless entry and the glassless windows. Anything the wind or animals or people could have taken has been taken long ago, and only congealed detritus and the structure and its foundations remain. Inside is a cafeteria with rows of benches and a rostrum to host announcements. The woman who arrived with us took to the stage and shouted over our excitement as we grabbed our seats. She called each of us who had misbehaved up and listed our infractions in front of everyone. Another dead end. A memory which leads back or to no other.

A Beacon in the Light

The wooden benches are now shattered remnants of their former selves, stuck to the floor by years of rain deposits. I stumble through them, my footfalls and the skittering shards of wood and glass saying something of entrapment here, except for the doorway behind me. I head toward the eastern wall until my hands runs against the metallic surface of the food line. A maze of dents on the metal panels where bats and two-by-fours and stones were used to vandalize them. The glass partisan is shattered. I trace along to the end of it. A few paces beyond it should be a single-door exit that opens to an outside deck. Something brings to mind rain coming down out there like an omen. I go to the door and shoulder it open and step out but my foot finds only air. I'm able to catch myself on the doorsill before falling. The oaken deck is gone, and it's now a four-foot drop to mud and weeds. I wait there for something to come to mind that might bring me out of here. But why would anything come? If it were easy to conjure the memories in any place without the places or people themselves, I'd have never returned. So, I stand and go back to the food line, and if there were trays I would have grabbed one to mime the business of getting food but there are no trays. From the quiet comes the static of some numeration of neurons picking through the silence for stimuli, creating it where there is none. A voice almost heard, an apparition almost seen... but nothing manifests. There must be something here! Or, against all else that happened, have I forgotten much of my time at camp? I fan my hands out over the metal and past the shattered partitions, knocking a plastic ladle to the floor.

The lunch guy uses it to slap a pile of steamed green beans onto my tray, then urges me down the line with a little nudge of his chin. All over his arms are sickly green tattoos and the lobes of his ears are stretched out like rubber bands. If this is a place for troubled kids it's so for some of the adults here. The guy down the line tonging meat-pucks onto trays is a worrisome character all his own. He's got a hairnet on without any hair. But what I'm certain has found its way into the food by now is the sweat dripping from his face. Some of the other kids have noticed this too and one asks him if he needs a towel or a smoke break. We're all sopping wet ourselves from the rain outside, and it's overcrowded in here with everyone seeking shelter from it all at once.

There's a group of girls in line behind me and one of them suggests she can read minds. She says she can guess what all the boy's are thinking of her, what I'm thinking. I ignore her, since pretending to be aloof is my only defense when responding in time is impossible. The group of girls had cut the line in a little huddle of whispers. The loud one is there to discourage objections, I suppose. And one of them keeps latching onto my backpack. I sway back and forth hoping she'll get the picture but she never does. "He's thinking, 'is she talking about me?'" I turn to her. She has dark hair and blue eyes and knows how pretty she is. The girl latched to my backpack is very small. Her dark blonde hair, gray eyes, and pale skin don't contrast so strikingly as the other girl's features, but she's pretty in her own right.

A Beacon in the Light

She holds herself a little off-center with her head tilted to the side and her hair covers much of her face like a shroud. Her features show vaguely from underneath, like through a window screen into a dim interior. She won't look away. I think I'm being tested somehow, measured by them. And look now: the little smile is gone from the face of the obnoxious brunette and the interest disappears from the eyes of the tawny blonde one, too. Witnessed in real time. I have the urge to insult them, to defend myself, but how? Against what? The dark-haired girl looks at me like I've transformed into something dangerous, teasing nothing more from me, clear she wants only to survive what remains of this encounter.

Someone cuts the line ahead. A boy taller than me, trying to look mean. Him I can fight, so I tug at his backpack and he turns and smacks my hand away. I grab his throat and he tries to push me off and we fall. Others circle around us chanting. We achieve little beyond dirtying our clothes, and after some embarrassing seconds of rolling around, a couple counselors rush over and pry us apart, one of them dragging me away by my collar up a flight of stairs and into an empty room.

I stay where I am. The recollection would have me sit in that room picking out the words spoken to me from the silence for hours. There's no time for that, and there's more here at my fingers: scratch marks on the metal. I'd sharpened the edge of a quarter, and one day used it to score the thin metal surface of the foodline. Why? Why not? My contribution to the decay here. The lunch guy saw me do it and made a fuss, and the counselor who'd broken up the fight days before was making her way through the isles toward me. I ran out the double doors. Large doors you could drive a tractor through.

I go to them and find the handles chained and padlocked together. The window to the left will do, since the particle board blocking it has already been battered down. I climb through and follow the rounding sidewalk to the Boys' Barracks, this, stenciled in white military font below the fascia. The barracks are two longhouses arranged side-by-side. The one I'd stayed in is boarded up like everything else. The handle is missing from the front door and there's wood nailed to the other side. A funnel web spider occupies the shallow recess where the handle was. My fingers tear the thick webbing and the occupant bats them away with its forelegs. I trace the building to the other side and stand still in search of any recollection that will take me north. Scattered imaginings, and then the pools, ersatz green in the sunlight. We came out from the barracks in our swimming shorts and towels draped over our shoulders and we followed the counselor over a field of trimmed grass. Unkempt now.

We come to a fence around the pool and a group of older kids are eyeing us from the water. The counselor, Ms. Hess, opens the gate and we enter the pool area. Heavy rain has replaced much of the treated water, turning it a pale green and there are little dunes of sediment laying at the bottom. I drape my towel on one of the long chairs and get into the water. It's cold, but not like the surrounding lakes. Everyone's in the shallow end, and one by one we're selected to swim the length of the pool under the water without coming up for air, so they know we won't drown or something. All the other kids have made it so far. I've swam plenty off my dock but never any great distance. It comes to my turn and I go under and immediately have the urge to breathe, but keep swimming. Tracking along on the bottom of the pool is the shadow of the lifeguard walking along the side above me. I'm about halfway across and still swimming fine, when, sooner than expected, my hand rakes the end of the pool and I burst out of the water for air. I look back at the other kids, but they don't care. Too nervous, themselves.

I climb out of the water and make my way back to the group of other kids waiting in the shallow end. There's a green plastic mesh fence separating the boy's pool from the girl's. Through it I see the small tawny haired girl from the other day, standing next to the shallow end. She's next in line to swim and looks afraid. The other girls are putting up masks of bravery, but she has both her hands cupped to her mouth and her arms are tucked at her sides. She doesn't look to the adults or anyone for encouragement, and only stares into the water. The counselor tells her to get in and she obeys, keeping hold of the side. She's told to swim and she takes a breath and goes under. Her pale form kicks frantically but moves hardly at all, despite the effort. The counselor pads along, looking around like she couldn't be bothered. The girl doesn't even make it halfway before coming up for air, coughing, her hair darkened and the volume of it pressed out like the coat of a cat who had fallen into the bathtub. She climbs from the pool and is directed to a bench where she sits holding herself.

Shards of coping break under my weight and skitter down the walls of the empty pool into a tepid puddle. The concrete pavers are cracked and some are missing. I walk the edge to the locker rooms; gone but for the concrete foundation and a rusted perron. Nothing about them comes. I'd elected against most pool activities in favor of the bow range, which is directly north of here.

I walk the field between the pools and the ranges. Piles of ash and little tipis of combustibles everywhere, much of it burnt to charcoal billets. Circles of tamped brush around them. I skirt these, but run instead into haphazard stacks of debris yet to be burned. In the stacks are the remains of the wooden benches from the Common Lodge and other shattered remnants of furniture. It's like someone wanted to erase all evidence that anyone once lived here at all, one piece at a time.

Beyond the field are saplings, young and flexible, and soon I step onto a metal sign that once instructed entrants on proper bow-handling etiquette. The posts stand rusted and bent. Someone tried to dig one of them up, only to find the eighty-pound cement block beneath it. The kiosk where the instructor dolled out bows and the arrows is gone, probably broken down and immolated in one of the fire piles in the field. Straw from hay bales is strewn everywhere. Cloth from the targets worked thoroughly into the clay. Sometimes my foot catches on the cloth and I drag it along, revealing the length of its network in the mud like pulling at the strands of a spider's web to reveal its invisible and frightening expanse.

Something stirs in the copse beyond the archery range. The animal lets out a low wretch. It's a raccoon. I ford into the thicket of black spruce thwacking the pines free of moisture and the animal scurries off somewhere, grousing its departure. The sound is a reminder of the quiet which must be maintained, and I stop moving to let the animal settle down someplace. The hunters could be near enough to hear it. That dog of theirs has been reigned in but it brought them to the road and to this place. It's best to assume they're always within earshot.

When it's quiet again I go on, my hand placed on the stem of the nearest tree stem, then the next, until ahead of me is an open field. I never went over it, only around, out of fear of being taken in by whatever sport was going on there. I'm anxious still, so I keep to the line of trees which goes to an ancient riverbed that hasn't run with water longer than I've been alive. A divide sits in the middle of it. We called it Giant's Tooth. Grykes you can walk through; you can fall through. Cavernous areas below where kids would shout up into the light and those above would shout down into the dark. A nature-made jungle gym. The danger of it lending to its appeal.

I cross the river bed and hike the chine of the divide to the formation of ironstone at its heights. It's not something that changes in just a couple decades, and it sits in darkness how it did in the light of day all those years ago; the shadow of pine swaying over one of its dozen entrances. With outstretched arms I come to it in the dark. The stone is cold and smooth and little rills trickle down from some reservoir of rainwater above. A labyrinth of turns and of odd-angled halls and those eternally enshadowed corners where bats take flight into the darkness. In one manifold hidden in darkness and crawling with arachnids, I sit and remove my backpack and put it on a rock shelf out of the wet, then lie down in that cold and musty place. The pain from a dozen small injuries comes at last. Adrenaline and constant moving had staved it for hours, and now at rest it's like a fine needle has finally shivered its way to something sensitive in my spine and impinges the workings. Just a moment's rest and I cannot move at all. The arachnids return. Cellar spiders plucking the hairs of my arms, my eyelashes. Nothing to do about it.

I sleep in brief grasps and dream no further than where I lie.

Voices glancing off the walls. They sound very near, about to duck the low jagged corner and find us here, but they never do. There's light enough to see and I pocket the flashlight and we sit together. The only light now is a blue gem of sky above, and a luminous vain of platinum sunlight on the wall. Neither of us speaks for a while. We're silent for most of the time we spend together. Bad at talking, the both of us, since we have no genuine commonalities and nothing interesting to say. I make do sometimes by borrowing stories from other people's lives: stories my father told about exploring scary places overseas and the like.

I'm ashamed to admit it was Lily who first talked to me. I was in the Common Lodge when she came over to tell me I had a pine beetle on my back. When I plucked it off I just started reciting a bunch of crap about the things. Maybe I'd seen or read something about pine beetles or some other beetle that I was drawing from, but really, I made most of it up. That was last summer, and Lily has since adopted an interest in bugs, and now we tell each other stories of those we've seen in the wild. I used to lie often to keep talking. I know that's bad, but I've found that it's some great sin to stop talking in the presence of a girl. The original sin, actually, when Adam had taken too long just looking at Eve like an idiot so she left to find better company with a snake.

I don't have to lie so much now, having kept an eye out for them. "I saw it on the side of my neighbor's boat. It looked like a stick until it started moving," I say and mime this with my arms.

"Why didn't you get it?"

"I would have hurt it. Last time I caught one it held on so tightly to the tree that I tore one of its legs off."

"Why didn't you take a picture?"

Shrugging: "I could have, but the pictures aren't for me, and my parents wouldn't be interested in a stick bug," I tell her. "They want me to take pictures of my friends and nice places."

Lily wraps her arms round her legs and looks at

her feet and she wiggles her toes in her sneakers. She's already small, but always makes herself smaller by collapsing in on herself. I think she'd prefer to fold herself up inside a shell or an acorn if she could do it. "You've never taken a picture of me," she says.

I blush. I want to make a joke of it somehow, but what would be the use of that? I'm finally alone with her and all I do is treat her like another boy. I breathe and decide to take her picture – thank god I chose that – and I get the Polaroid out from my backpack and point it at her and she opens up a little, sits upright and lets go of her legs then rests her hands on her knees. She smiles in her way, so feint it's almost like it isn't a smile at all. I take the photo and it rolls out of the slot. Lily grabs it before I can and waits for it to develop. I think she wants me to scoot in closer but I don't, and just watch as she tilts her and lets her hair fall from behind her shoulders around her face. Her eyes flick over the emerging elements in the picture and at me like sharp things to be wary of. She is something to be feared and something to give your life for at once.

Someone speaks. They know and in the dark they say her name and tell me to keep her close. To hold her hand. They say to take her and run, and I do, never tiring.

Aaron

Firelight shimmers through the trees. Emergency lights.

It's a pickup in the middle of the trail fully engulfed in flames. The others dispatched here arrived before I did and called it in just ten minutes ago.

I roll up and pan my halide about the burning vehicle, looking for prints or what have you. From the firetruck a nozzle team approaches with a pressurized hose and the lead man opens it up to douse the flames and the nearby trees in a cone of water, narrowing it into a beam to chisel at the blackened remains of the vehicle. The fire is gone in seconds. They cut the hose and watch for a while, talking among themselves. They seem to see something and they radio that there are propane tanks in the bed that might bleve any second. Then, after some deliberation they decide it's safe, and go to the ruined truck with fire hooks and pick at the fabric seats for hidden embers that might reignite the pools of mud and gasoline mixture around the melted tires. The fuel tank had been punctured and its contents set alight on purpose, that much is clear. No owner to be found.

Chatter cracks over my radio about a body found on the trails nearby. Male, thirty-something, Caucasian. A simple search and rescue right to the scene of a murder, just like that. Then again, isn't that always how these things go?

A search team emerges from the darkness of the woods at the limits of my headlights. Sean Webb is with them. I climb from the Jeep and meet them at the hood. "Body is fifty yards off the trail," says Webb. "Looks dragged, like someone meant to throw it in with the truck and burn them together. Probably ran when they saw us coming. I think they might be close."

"ID?"

"No one's looked for one, but I'm guessing no." Webb gets in his wide stance like he's preparing for the ground to move under him. "There's more: we found a dog. A German Shepherd with a harness, rifle shot through the neck. My guy didn't have a dog." He looks at me.

"Guess we know who it is, then," I say.

"We've got tracks going in all directions," says Gibbs. "Let's be careful not to ruin them with ours."

I nod and climb back into the Jeep and radio for canine teams. Sean and the photographer and Gibbs are all looking in through the windshield at me. Maybe they think I'd want to see the body myself. I suppose I do, but I'm all out of step, missing beats, fumbling like a guy caught tossing the murder weapon. I already called for Canine teams.

I rejoin them.

"Prayer break?" asks Sean Webb.

The body is tucked into a little crook, arms akimbo and legs crossed in the manner of a crucifix. The face is chewed to hell. Lacerations everywhere. Bloodless though, like it's a mannequin. He looks to be in his early or mid-thirties, same as William, but everything else is wrong. Skin is all gray and the neck is bloated. This body is a week old at least. "I think he's your guy," I tell Sean.

"You want to roll him, get at his back pockets?" asks Gibbs. He slaps at a mosquito on his neck.

"I don't want to touch him."

A forensics team is flagging evidence deeper in the woods, their flashlights combing the darkness and casting opposing shadows of the woods. We go to them. In the leaves lies the dead Shepherd. Poor girl could be sleeping but for the line of blood braiding down her neck to the mud. Her collar is missing. So are her ears. "Girl was mauled."

"Like the other guy," says Webb.

I put on a pair of blue latex gloves and click on a pen light and peel back the dog's lips. Wet tufts of fur caught between the teeth. "Good girl. She returned in kind. Look."

Webb kneels. Nods. "The other one'll be leaking all over the place. Probably a better trail than the men it belongs to."

"We don't have dogs trained to track other dogs," I say. Sean and I stand. My knees crack loudly.

"So what the hell you suppose happened out here?" he asks.

I turn to the surrounding darkness. The vague apparitions of trees like a crowed come to gawk at the newly dead. "I'm thinking that dog brought William to the corpse over there. I'm thinking we'll find his body not far from here."

Webb nods then he says, "you gonna tell the girl we found her dog?"

"What's the need?" I ask him.

"Something about bringing her around to it?"

"We'll find him soon. Might as well give it to her all at once."

He shrugs.

In the mud are tracks crossed over each other, each one stake-flagged with different colors in accordance to their logic. Three distinct sets so far. It was a fight. Body imprints everywhere. A knee. An elbow patterned with the folds of fabric. From the furball the tracks continue north and we follow and meet up with two guys making headway. "Chief," greets one. We gather around, taking care not to contaminate the tracks with our own. "Notice anything about them?" the man says.

"They're the same."

"Yeah, but we're definitely dealing with more than one person. They've probably got bags around their shoes. Grass, foliage stuffed into them."

I kneel and angle my light almost parallel to the ground and indeed, there's no tread to them at all. William's prints are easy to pick out from the others, but it seems effort was taken to tamp them down as to confuse his heading. Near to the tracks is an object glinting with the light of my flashlight. The forensics guys haven't spotted it yet. It's a collapsed cane for the blind and I motion its location to the others. "He'd need that to get far," says Webb, and does a once over of the area like the body should be strung up in the trees nearby in a barbaric display.

"Dog tracks. Look," says Gibbs. He pans his light over a galloping pattern of them. We follow into another patch of mud but it isn't clear where the chase had continued on. It's another furball. No body prints this time. "They ran him down," he says. "Then they scattered like roaches."

"I don't think so," says Webb. "This is supposed to confuse us. Look how they loop around." He traces what he sees with his light but I don't see what he does.

One of the forensics guys curses about his back then begins flagging them, and all of us work to untangle the tracks from one another. Sean was right, this was certainly an attempt to confuse police on where the pursuit continued from here. There are three separate paths of them going off into the surrounding woods. I tell Sean and Gibbs we'll have to follow every one.

"Fine, but what's our approach here?" asks Gibbs. "These look pretty fresh. They're closer than I'm comfortable with and I doubt they'll let us walk up on 'em."

"Oh, they're gone," says Webb, yet he takes his pistol from its holster and chambers a round then holsters it again. The canine teams arrive in their Tahoes. I take the time to get something appropriate for the task from my Jeep: a Mossberg loaded nine plus one and I grab the shirt Jessica gave me. We meet back at the maze of tracks and I brief the canine teams and give them the shirt and they give the scent to the dogs, smothering their snouts in the garment. Each of the five bloodhounds go at once to the ground to pick out the scent, pacing back and forth. There's no call for them to begin, but a beginning develops over the course of some minutes, when, as if a hare suddenly leaped from one of the bushes, they bound forth without warning. We follow with our handheld or weapon-mounted lights pointed in all directions. Gun holsters and radios clacking in unison – the cacophony you could hear in the dark and still know that it came from policemen in pursuit. The hounds are silent as they work ahead of us. We're going strong for half a minute when they begin to wander, sweeping here and there from interest to interest. Seems the scent-trail ends here, but there's no indication of an end such as a body or sign of struggle. The handlers take the dogs in loops. We search the ground at our feet but there's nothing to find. Forensics mark the area with flags and on maps and we wait for the dogs to agree on another direction. When they do, we follow them to an expanse of switchgrass and pale birch trees, many fallen and lying orthogonal to those yet to fall, like the raw framework of homes put up then abandoned. Here, the hounds lose and pick up scent-trails over and over, crossing and recrossing between each other and doing a good job trampling any prints that might be on the ground. They don't continue on, but one of them has closed in on a fallen birch tree, tracing the length of it with its keen nose. An old dog, gray at the snout and experienced. "I got something here," says the handler. He rolls the log over with his foot and orders the hound to sit on its haunches. Under the log are clusters of pill bugs and a scarf. Probably William's. "Suppose that's on purpose," he remarks.

"I suppose so."

"It was a long shot anyway." The man swigs from a water bottle. "Area is too contaminated."

All the men gather around waiting. I guess they're waiting for instruction, so I step into the center of them letting the Mossberg hang by its strap and tell them we'll do a sweep with cadaver dogs. "In the meantime, everyone watch for prints and flag what you find. Be careful where you step. This may be our only chance to get an idea where it is they're going." Everyone gives some affirmative.

Braids of rain streak through the beams of our lights like bolides. Sparse at first, stopping briefly before coming down in a deluge. I start back to the Jeep alone, with my light at the ground, the edges and peaks of everything glimmering in the wet. Leaves, twigs, and... a single boot print, tread and all. Oriented north, looks fresh. There's no doubt about it, has to belong to William.

Only seconds have passed and I haven't missed even a heartbeat's time before I tamp down the print down with my own. So small an act I don't really feel it. Maybe it's the only tell of where the chase had gone on or maybe not. Someone else might come across more prints and this moment will be as meaningless as it feels.

Either way, what remains unrecorded in light for those long-from-now observers are thoughts. They will see and think I'm a fool, and that's okay.

I emerge on the trail and climb into the Jeep and lay the shotgun on the passenger seat then sit awhile peering through the window with my heart thundering. All through the dark forest there are lights flicking at the shadows as if to defend against them. Were any of them near enough to see me? I try to imagine the inverse paths of those lights, running it all back on rewind. Surely, I was alone. No one could have been near enough to see what I did – what I did without thought, like driving or chewing gum.

There's no other place I need to be, but I won't stay here, and I fire up the engine and drive with the rain thwacking the windshield. The dark sketches of men make way ahead, standing at the edges of my headlights and looking on like black rooks sheltered in the trees.

William

Lucid dream after dream; of things that happened, things I wish happened or am glad did not. A developing discomfort carries from each to the next; is incorporated into them somehow. The discomfort is an itching fire that grows on my left arm and spreads to the hand I use to scratch at it.

Fully awake now, the cold morning air stinging my eyes, I realize that I've slept on a colony of fire ants. They're all over me and inside the seams of my pants, biting hot lines where the fabric hugs too tight for them to squeeze past. I brush them off and grind the rest between my skin and the fabric. The movement reveals more injuries. A few small lacerations on my arms and face reopen and my fingers become wet with blood. There's no time to dress them so I tend to the possibility of a sprained elbow, probably from tumbling into the osier. I grab compression wrap from the medical kit in my backpack and wrap it several times until taut. It's not much, but it helps some with the pain. I bat around for my things and decide to take stock of what I lost fleeing. The white cane, scarf, and my cell is busted. Screen shattered and the whole thing is bent in the middle. The battery is probably compromised, but it's not like I'd have signal out here, anyway.

I've still got the backpack with water and some items of food. There's a thermal blanket in one of the inside pockets. Chrome colored I believe, maybe orange. Meant to be seen anyway, from far off, so using it in the open is out of the question.

With that I gather everything up and toss the broken phone on the ground and grab the rifle with my good arm. Then I trace along the stone walls, water uttering its descent into cold immaculate puddles on the ground. A breeze calls the way out in turbulent fricatives and I make my way there through the maze of narrow corridors. At the exit, I pause and listen, searching with the ears outward to find only the groaning pine and waking birds. The sun hasn't risen yet, and it's still very cold.

I step from the grykes of Giant's Tooth onto a pine-strewn declivity. All scrutiny arrayed at me and none the reverse, and the numb eyes of the wild find nothing of itself reflected in mine. If it could surmise it might that I'm something caught in the wind, and I move just so; quiet and light as a leaf. The rocky divide ends at the spurn of an elm tree, and I'm back on the riverbed. It's impossible to move as quietly as before in the loose rocks. The stones the size and shape of eggs that chatter against one another – language informed by such sounds and they say the names of themselves.

I follow the defilade of the old river for some minutes when I'm turned from it by some recognition: sifting through the oval river rocks for interesting ones to take home, raking up handfuls and tossing most of them away. "What'cha got there?" said a boy, and then a stone smacked down in the pebbles next to me. It was meant to hit me, and had come from the bank where a crooked plain of thin pine went up from the rivercut. So uniform in its ascent that you lose the orientation of it wholesale, and the kinesthesia of your body too, and it becomes as likely you've gone crooked rather than the land. On this stood a tall boy on a mossy boulder of granite. He was perhaps a year older than I was. His spine was off, and it struck me at once that the id of him had been shaped around the deformity as my own around impending blindness. He had four others with him and all looked down at me motionless until one took up another rock and pitched it at me. He missed again. I didn't move. They took that as a challenge and all began hurling stones my way to make little craters all around me, but all missed. I scampered out of arm's-throw then. They hadn't spoken a word and neither had I. There came shouting from the rocky divide behind me, and a group of kids joined me. Myself and three others stared up at the group of antagonizers until one of the kids near to me shouted that they should join us down here, and that we should fight if a fight is what they wanted. What I wanted was to run. The kid who challenged them spoke in an accent I'd never heard before. His skin was moonlight pale. He looked more athletic than me.

The crooked kid and his pals came down and the four of us, allied spontaneously, stood opposite them. Two held rocks in their hands and I wondered if they really intended on using them, or if it was meant for intimidation. The pale kid nudged my arm and at some point I don't recall, the fight ensued. An awkward affair. Some short and fat kid charged me ass first, I suppose to guard his head, and when I was in range he wheeled around and swung at me. It was as humiliating to witness as it was to get caught by, but that happened only once, and then I just kicked the back of his knees and he fell down, then stood and squared up to box it out. I hardly recall how that went, adrenaline dulling the pain and the memory. We didn't have the strength to do real harm to each other, save for those rocks, and the kids holding them had thrown them and had missed. We rolled around awhile numb to it all. I was decked square on the nose and was glad to find it didn't hurt at all, though I bled some. The determination on the faces of the agitators vanished when they knew we wouldn't run. Not a win but not a loss either, and that was good enough. We heard the counselors shouting from the trees and scattered, myself and the pale kid dashing into a treeline opposite the campgrounds and we hid in the bracken. This way...

Their voices came near and we ducked low in the leaves. A woman and a man grabbed what kids they could and dragged them back toward camp. Most of them who were caught had been with us. The instigators ran for it.

"What's your name?" the kid asks.

"Avery."

"You kick ass, Avery."

"You too."

"Hakon."

"What's that?"

"My name. Where should we go?" He's a bit shorter than me, but certainly stronger. We listen a while. The counselors search and come close and we don't dare to look out from hiding to catch the sight of them. Their eyes and voices sweep over us and we stay low. When they turn and leave and are far enough Hakon says, "We should get back before them."

"Yeah. We'll keep to the woods."

He nods and runs off ahead of me, waving me to follow.

I stay. No good backtracking, so I turn in search of anything else that will take me away from them, further north. Indeed, I had stood someplace near here, on a slope looking out over the riverbed. And on the opposing side there were three gray wolves weaving through the trees, looking to me like background stage elements in a play. It had all gone flat with my right eye nearly blind entirely by this time. They stopped and held at the bole of a tall coniferous tree where at the top an eagle's nest was perched. Nestlings bobbing and flapping their premature wings. Three in number. The wolves sat and waited, looking up at the nest and making no sound. The mother eagle came over, its shadow projected through a thin fog and cast on the ground as it circled and came down to the nest with a small fish in its claw. It shook its head and the feathers blossomed out and then it tore at the fish and gave the pieces out to the chicks but for one of them. Smaller and frailer than its siblings. The chick was given no food and when the fish had been dolled out to the others the mother eagle plucked the reject by its neck and dropped it from the nest to the wolves below. They didn't at once devour it, but smelled the baby bird and rolled it around with their snouts until the larger of them opened its jaws in a slow smile and clamped them down around the neck of the nestling. The others each took a wing and pulled it apart like something made of paper mache.

It's a blank after that, the memory, and I doubt there's much more to remember of this place. Should I chance going north anyway? What happens if I get lost? What happens is I'm caught and killed. So, with even less time now, I turn and follow at last.

Hakon and I kept to the protection of the trees. We were in a hurry, but now I must take care not to make too much noise, and I go slowly through the brambles and the papery leaves. Some minutes of walking, and a silence settles all around me, or what I thought was a silence until ahead of me extended a truer sense of this, a more complete absence of sound than what I'd taken as it before. The absolute notion, where there's nothing to hear on closer concentration. Then, out over a sward of tall grass where the foundations of the barracks lie, comes the clip of claws on the concrete. It's that dog, Ban. It's handlers bring it around the barracks, corner to corner. If they look this way, they'll see me standing here among the trees like some frightened doe in the road. Maybe they already have.

I step backwards into the treeline, toes first, rolling onto the heel, back where hanging branched grasp at my clothes and conceal me. I press through, deeper, rustling them like a breeze, and when I'm sure there's enough foliage between us I turn and walk faster with distance. The way becomes familiar. It's in the way that the ground lopes like waves. There should be a trail not far to my left, headed by a totem sculpture made from the stem of a pine tree. I turn there and follow it, but stay within the trees until the path veers left at a clearing for some expansion of the campgrounds that never came. After the bend, I go out onto the trail and follow it half a mile before it sweeps down into a valley that's part of the old riverbed. I'm quick across, and pick up the trail again on the other side where it winds to an end at the base of an ancient aspen. I've made good distance, so there's time enough to think; to elicit some recollection.

Old logs lie half-buried under the duff around the aspen. Three rows of them, enough for a small congregation. The place was called Shouting Tree. One of the camp counselor named Huston brought us here for some attempt at a group therapy session. He had the look of a recovering addict, or like he didn't care how he looked except to the extent that it might be inappropriate to look any worse. His ratty beard was the color of his skin and his eyes seemed perpetually irritated. He wore khaki shorts and a white tee with the camp logo, but also he wore a long moss green scarf made of some light material that took easily in the breeze.

He claimed the dead aspen was killed by the bad energies of angry and bitter children in the past. He told us it's *our* job to coax it back to life by giving it positive energy. But, that's only possible if we get all our hate out on it first. "It's already dead, so give it all you got," he told us. We did our best, and he said to pay attention to our emotion and notice its power on others and ourselves, or some crap like that, but we just laughed. Who hired this hippie, anyway?

Afterwards, we finish the ritual by giving it our compliments, begrudgingly, and Huston then assured us that by this time tomorrow it'll have come back to life. He was right! Returning today, there are now all these tiny green bulbs sprouting from what brambles the tree has left. But, I'm certain they were already there. It's just that yesterday we were kept too far from the tree to see them.

We repeat the exercise as before, a little rowdier this time. Most of us make do poking fun at the whole thing, ejecting obscenities and such, but some of us go in at the hippie orchestrating the nonsense. Someone tells him he smells like dead rats, and I guess he's had enough, so he raises his hands like a preacher taken by the spirit to quiet us down. He says he doesn't mind those of us who would say the worst, but he's concerned about those of us who say nothing out of fear of what they *might* say. He's going to make an example of one of us, and he'll choose someone who can't fight back. His sunken eyes go over us and linger on those he thinks were too silent and, finally, they rest on Lily. She was only miming the words, even the compliments. I can pick her voice from a crowd easily, so I know.

"What's your name?" he asks her. Everyone is dead silent now.

"Lily."

"Lily what?"

"Lily McLloyd."

"What are you afraid you might say, Lily McLloyd?" To this she says nothing and the man says, "Are you thinking up a lie to tell me?" She shakes her head, the gesture bringing her hair around her face and she doesn't brush it aside. "You won't speak your mind? You have nothing to say at all? Or do you think this is stupid? That I'm stupid?" Lily nods. He laughs. "Okay. Tell me I'm stupid."

"You're stupid," she says without hesitation. Everyone laughs.

"Good. And what else?"

She thinks for a while, then she says, "You're a liar. The sprouts were on the tree yesterday. You just kept us further away hoping we didn't see them."

"Very good. What else?"

"There's nothing else."

"Do you hate it here?"

"Oftentimes."

"Do you want to go home?"

"No."

"So you hate being here. You hate being home.

Where do you like to be?"

"Anywhere I don't have to be."

"Ah, a free spirit. In that case you may go," he says. She looks around then she shrugs. "So you don't hate it here all that much?"

"I just have no other place to go to."

"Did your parents make you come here?"

"I asked to come."

"Did you think it would be different?"

"No. I knew it would be something like school."

Huston winces. "Ouch, our camp is something like school?" He asks this of us all. A mixture of answers. Honest answers. Nobody wants to fling out insults or obscenities any longer. "Well, it seems we have some improvements to think about here."

"This place is for troubled kids isn't it?" asks Lily.

"Not really, no. But it seems something about our marketing attracts the kind." A few of the others laugh. Lily smiles. Something leaps from my mouth. I hardly hear what. It was something really bad though, and Huston looks baffled; taken by total surprise this time. I want the others to join in but they don't and some even gawk at me. Hakon, always having my back, starts shouting his own insults, and since he commands more approval than I do, more of us join in. Some reclamation there, but not much. Lily looks humiliated.

There's nothing after that, nothing I can use to leave here, anyway. The aspen remains. Its bark is brittle and lifeless. God, what was it I said?

A quarter-mile away, Ban lets out a chocked

shriek. At this rate I'll run short of imaginings to follow and they'll be right behind me for that moment, and that moment is near. I'm armed, but they'll soon realize that I'm no threat with or without the weapon, and they'll come.

No choice now.

I go northwest, blind. Pine trees hushing in the wind above. I've lost count of the minutes, but it's not long before I trample over an old deer kill, cracking through the rib cage with my foot. Disturbing the bones wafts their scent into the air; of musky decay and urine, too. Very pungent. Could I use it to obscure my own scent somehow? Probably not, but a related idea hits me, and I take up what feels like a femur bone and use it to dig out a small trench in the earth near the old kill. By the sound of that dog, I have maybe five minutes before they're on me, so I'll have to be quick.

The trench dug, I compare the length of the rifle against it and dig out some more till they match, then I fit the rifle into the trench at a slight angle upwards, digging out more dirt as needed to accommodate the stock. The hound nears.

With that done, I remove the boot and sock from my left foot and pack the sock with handfuls of leaves. Then I pat the ground for a stick or for a bone of the right length, splaying out my hands and rowing them over the ground. Finding nothing, I stand and reach out and walk a ways than catch the hanging foliage of a maple tree. The twigs are healthy and bend too easily, but on the ground near its base are the molted members dried over the months or years since they'd fallen. I snap a length from a larger branch and rip the clinging leaves from it and, counting my paces back, return to where I dug the trench and measure the stick from the trigger of the rifle along the barrel. It extends maybe three inches past the nozzle, and that'll do just fine.

With a pocket knife I cut a little dado at one end of the stick like the knock of an arrow and test this against the trigger and find it snug. With the stick running parallel to the barrel I slide my sock over the nozzle and the stick then place the rifle into the little trench and situate it so the stock is solid against the hard clay and the nozzle protrudes from the ground. I feel for the trigger and fit the notched end of the stick against it and slide it down to the point of the trigger, till only a slight pressure will set it off, then I cover it all with leaves.

They're close, a hundred meters away at best and closing the distance fast. I slide my boot back on and stand and head directly west, or what I think is west, rushing through the hanging branches and uneven terrain like a mad fool and making all kinds of noise and scattering the duff like a stampede came through. The hound is barking and thrashing wildly. So close – right back there where I had been just a minute ago! It whines and draws a haggard breath. No shouting from the men, not yet. How is it they don't hear me? Are they making too much noise themselves? Have they passed it? Of course they passed it! The dog is clapping its jaws with excitement, gurgling through its constricted trachea. Now it's raking its claws over the earth in a sudden burst of speed! Oh god!

Then... there's the whip-crack of a gunshot. I drop to the ground, listening. Nothing. No pain either. The dog has been reined-in or it has been shot through the mouth. But they are close regardless. A short sprint away. I stand, keeping low, and go with nothing but the early sun on my back for direction.

<u>Jessica</u>

A fishing boat drifts out on the water, shadowed against the emerging daylight, its wake like the folds of copper-iron damascus. It disappears near to the shore where the waves rise and scatter the light of the sunrise too much to limn the boat any longer. Two docks down from ours an elderly woman breaks bread for loons and sqauils the pieces into the thick of them and they flap and dart energetically to take up the bread from which no nutrient is derived.

No sleep. Improper for me to sleep and improper to eat at a time like this. My phone is where I tossed it on the rocking chair next to the fireplace. I'd seen it on the news about a body found on Echo Trail and called Police. I got through to Chief McLloyd and he assured me it wasn't William, though Moxie had been found dead close by. Shot by someone and now a manhunt is on. I've called William's phone but it goes to voicemail and so far that's all I've thought to do. Catatonia. Freeze response. I've not felt the despair yet, only frustration. But over what? It was me who instilled insecurity in him. I had witnessed him in a place he'd been to as a kid. A place he had seen when he could: Weavers Needle. I saw the difference it made and the way he stood and looked around and the way he moved, so differently than how he behaved in unfamiliar places. Things went stale after that. He felt it, and decided to come here not long after. I helped bring this on so I can't just sit here forever. That would be improper too.

I stand from the table and go into the spare room.

Piles of things. Tote boxes and old clothes. Start where? A display of bugs leaning against the wall behind one of the stacks of boxes. Two by two feet wide. Rare moths pinned up behind the dusty glass. Indigenous, I think, and there's a space reserved at the top for a particularly large specimen. Could be William's or could be the previous owner's. Why is it here? Had the old owners never bothered to make something of this room? Why don't I know if William used to collect bugs?

I begin with the boxes. Old things. Clothes and odd trinkets that are mementos a parent places special importance on, but no child. Currency from places he'd probably never been to, and Freemason artifacts such as a golden penny with the Square and Compass symbol punched into it, and some filigreed lapels. In a cigar box are patinated shell casings from different kinds of weapons as well as rocks of all sorts. An uncut garnet gem. A nugget of asbestos. Yes, asbestos. It's certainly peculiar, the tiny carcinogenic crystalline fibers look like fur. A strange find for a kid, so I figure the cigar box must be things that William collected. Under the rocks is a stack of photos. The one on top is scratched dull and unrecognizable. The ones underneath were spared but are mostly pictures of nothing important. A few are of people. Children swinging into a river from a rope. Paddle boats. One of William and another child smiling. They seem to be in a large fissure between two sheer faces of gray stone. A dozen other children are standing above the fissure, extending their arms down into the chasm with all the melodrama of angels beckoning the damned to salvation.

I set the photo and the cigar box aside and move on. Newer clothes. A small t-shirt of Hemsworth's Thor. I see. The previous owners must have kept it all for their own son, and then they left some of their own belongings here.

Old jackets and over-shirts on the hanging rod in the closet. A squirt gun propped against the wall behind these. Super Soaker XP one-o-five. Three purple hopper tanks. The pump is gone. A red fishing pole next to it, the yellow line all tangled up at the mouth of the spool. Child-sized. A tackle box. Rusted lures and hooks inside and a pocket knife. Everything I touch looks and smells like it hasn't been moved in a long time, like the air settled around all the artifacts has gathered up trace amounts of them, of the plastics and metals and rubber. *Why* was it all left behind? Was there some need to get away as fast as possible?

More photos strewn among the stacks of discarded things. Wilderness. Nice places but nondescript. Sunsets. Reflections on water. A girl sitting at the end of a dock, facing out and silhouetted against a silver lake. Her hair flows down to the wooden boards and her legs dangle into the mirrored water like she'd been there long enough to let the ripples settle. On the upper corner the yellow font marks the date: "07/04/1999"

I set it aside.

In the closet is a target bow and several folded paper target shrouds with arrow-holes. Another t-shirt with "Slim Lake Camp" stenciled onto it. Summer Camp. Nineteen-ninety-nine. I stand at the center of the room holding the bow and the shirt and am glad the spirit of my own childhood does not lay as ashes in a room for someone to find.

I lay the bow and the shirt on the floor, and I can only think to search the browser on my phone for the camp and the year. Pictures of children posing in front of buses and a road sign. Where's the road? Five miles north of here. No roads go there anymore.

Articles about the Camp's closure and possible reopening, these dating back to two-thousand-seven. Stories of bodies found here over twenty years ago. The police were sure they'd find the killer but they never did. The articles offer no other insights. Vague assurances to the public. A sketch of a man. A boy? Looks like everyone and no one. Uncanny, like a skinwalker. A human face stretched over an inhuman skull. You'd meet the man and would never think to draw the relation. Then you'd be dead or on your way none the wiser. A sketch to reveal how contrived the practice is. Shapes put up, thrown up in some base pattern of human likeness. It looks like a million other faces. Sits in the middle of them as an aggregate. I go to the bathroom and compare, putting the image of the sketch on my phone beside my own reflection. See? It looks like me as much as anyone.

Feeling a little numb now, having stood still with my thoughts, I go into the living room, sit then stand again then dial the number of Chief McLloyd. The phone rings four times and the man answers as if by accident, static on the other end as he moves the phone from his pocket to ear. "Miss Albane?"

"I'm sorry to call you this early, but I have information that might be useful." I say it fast. Pleasantries cumbersome. I want to stamp the man's forehead with the completion of my thoughts and fall to bed.

"Alright. What information do you have for me?"

"I think William is going to Slim Lake Camp. He seems to have gone there as a kid."

There's no response for a while and then he says, "I appreciate the tip, always, but we're aware of the Camp and it doesn't look like he's going there at all."

"It's not possible for him to go anywhere else."

"I understand his limitations. But we need to be ready for other possibilities," he says.

A phrase intended to soften the blow of things to come. I want to throw the phone out the window. Instead I say, "Please tell me what you mean?"

The man holds silent on the line too long for anything but bad news to follow. "We've picked up a trail following Burntside's northern lakefront," he says.

"William looks to be among them. Evidence of someone being dragged. No blood, but he could be unconscious or bound so we're working fast to head them off. There's also the possibility we're being led away from him. A trick of theirs we've come to know."

I nod like he can see it.

"We'll find him, Miss Albane."

He left out whether they'll find him alive or dead. It's all the encouragement he can offer. I know this, but I'm too tired for tact so I ask him, "Could this have anything to do with what happened twenty years ago?"

He shifts the phone and says, "What makes you say that?"

"I'm not sure," I tell him. "In some parts of the city, people can be killed on the same street corner and none of them are connected. But out here it's different. Isn't that right?"

He breathes. "It's possible the same people are responsible. The case was abandoned."

"Were you on it? The case?"

"I was homicide, yes," he says. "We were unprepared. Ely was a small town then, but now we-" he does not go on. Silence on the line. Was he going to tell me they're prepared this time? A lie he can't bring himself to voice. "I have to go," he says all of a sudden. "We'll talk soon, alright?"

He ends the call. There's nothing left for me to do, no task to keep the despair away, and I rest my head on the table when it comes at last.

Aaron

There's a knock at the door and I pocket the phone. It's Webb, looking in at me through the glass. I motion for him to enter and he does, peering around at the arrangement of fit-lock rubber mats and the sleeping bag I spent the night in. "Was that the spouse?" he asks. I nod. "I just got off the phone with the dead's father."

"Is he coming down to ID?"

"I think. The man didn't say much but he made a noise in the affirmative, so I'll be leaving this to you." He walks to my desk and throws down his binder and whips it open. Leaving what to me? His suggestions on where next to look for William. "I'm guessing they'll toss the body somewhere on the north-western edge of Burntside."

"I've got a boat team there already."

"We'll need more than that. Three should do, for continuous coverage. And men posted up at the banks for mile in either direction."

"Yeah, but if they dump the body anywhere in the lake the current'll just take it up here, anyway," I point to the northernmost point of the lake.

"'Unless they anchor it."

"I don't think they'll anchor it," I say.

"Either way, the idea is to catch them in the act. Or you couldn't care less?"

I splay my hands to present the disarray of my office as evidence to the contrary.

"I don't know. You're fumbling around, hesitant,

then you fight me on everything," he says.

"You want me to snap to, is that it?"

"I want you to think, Chief."

"This is a waste of time."

"What is?"

"What we're doing now. I'm happy to work with you, but not against you."

Sean seems to bounce the notion around in his head. "If you say so."

"Any case, I agree. We'll get the extra boats, divers, and men as needed."

"Good," says Webb. He slaps his binder shut then goes for the door. "Maybe Dad can ID my guy in the meantime. Glean it from his silence anyway." He shuts the door and leaves it rattling behind him.

William

An hour plodding through a marsh. Overcast comes to block the sun and without it, I struggle to maintain a consistent direction. Slim Lake is supposed to be a mile from the campgrounds and I'm sure I've gone twice that. Sodden clay pulls at my heels and records my heading for the men to find and follow. I should assume as much anyway. It might be that the only reason I'm alive is because that rifle forced them to be cautious. I could have just shot at them as before, and thinking about it, that dog gave away their location as much as it did mine. Poor mutt. Then again, that thing attacked Moxie.

The wind slows and I hear better for it. A

beehive hums a ways to my right. Something large moves over piles of dead leaves. The sound of hooves clipping stone. It's a deer, and it runs when it hears me, going east, bounding high into the air and soon it treads water, tracing the edges of a lakefront. I follow. The sour smell of it comes first, then the rhythm of light waves folding onto coarse sand. I walk the beach and come to a tangle of branches curling into the lake. Too many to press through, so I tread into the shallow waves to avoid the thick of them. The water is cool. I drink from the straw of my pouch – empty – so I kneel and scoop away a film of rime on the water's surface, then bring a handful of it to my lips. Irony, bitter. It'll do. I open the bag and submerge the pouch till it's full then close it up and go on through the half-sunken canopy, batting through webs and entangling them between my fingers. The strong anchor threads pull across my face and the swift spiders skitter over my arms and leap into the water to seek ground somewhere. I slip a couple times on the mossy stones under the water, making a ruckus.

Nothing yet to spark a memory of this place, but imaginings come all the same: the gray-wooded dock that belongs to the strange cabin near my own where a berm of bur oak hangs over the water like claws. My mind wants to put me there like an obsessive thought looping around. But it's not possible that I've gone miles back to Burntside. I can't be there. See?

Blank at last.

Floating in the water are man-made things borne up on local gyres. Tarpaulin, nets, string and plastic containers, foam and cork floats and rusted soda cans that chime the progress of their disintegration. Past the detritus, I can hear the waves lapping against a set of lumber posts in the water. It was once a dock here, but now it's only those posts. And a little into the water there's a sunken paddle boat, slick with algae. The very same we used to get across the lake. It isn't that deep, or that far across. I could probably swim it, but I'd rather not chance swimming in circles and tiring out there.

I travel a mile or more of reeking beachfront to another set of docks where we shored the paddle boats. A rope swing was tied to the limb of an elm tree not far from where I stand now.

Still frames. Pictures, perhaps: a line of us snaking up the escarpment of brown rock; a boy swinging out over the amber water and shunting into it with hardly a splash; emerging, then dog-padded ashore to stand pale and slender in the sun. From some other time: Lily sat at the end of the dock with her toes in the cold water, limned by the specular surface – just a smeared shadow against the brilliance, but I know it's her. Give me a strand of hair or the arc of her hand magnified a hundred times. Give me one-thousandth of a second then flip the image on any axis and I'll pick her out from the noise. What I'm recollecting is in fact a photo taken in the final summer before I left for good. That year camp had been canceled, but Lily and I came to the rope swing by trail anyhow. I gave her that photo after I took it. She smiled and gave it back. What did I do with it?

The gangway is sunken a few inches beneath the water. It's twenty paces or so from it to a small shack slanted now on its foundations, the corrugated metal sheets shedding scales of rust on touch. From there, I hike the scarp to the rope swing and stand there feeling the empty air for it but there's nothing. Under the tree begins a foot trail, scored over by the tracks of animals and flattened by rain, but some boundary to it remains. I follow it northbound.

From the right of me, should be east, comes the low throb of a helicopter. The land plays on the echo of it circling halos in the sky, and sometimes it sounds close then it sounds far away again and then it's gone wholesale and for good. If they're looking for me, it seems they can't imagine that I've made it this far northeast.

The sun is low. A flight of bats above, their chirping like the minute ticking of a bad bought of tinnitus. Thirty minutes on the trail. Night comes with a portrait of a rocky jut of land under the arcature of the Milky Way and the sky the color of plums. The moon and the stars are all pinned up on crosses of their own light.

"What's wrong with taking a long time?" says Lily.

"If you don't care then I don't," I say. She goes silent and starts to meander from one fringe of the trail to the other. "Won't your folks?" I ask her.

She shrugs. "It doesn't matter. What about yours?"

"They'd ask and I'd tell them I was making sure a friend got home okay."

She was walking as if under water, and with her arms folded in front and her hair voluminous and the white dress wimpling in the breeze, she took on the image of an apparition on the darkened trail that a traveler some distance off might later say was an omen to beware.

"What would they say to that?" she asks.

"They would ask what kind of friend needs so much attention, and I'd say 'the girl kind' and they'd get real nosy about it."

She looks back at me. "It's not a good idea for me to go back at night. It's better if I go tomorrow during the day."

"What's the time of day got to do with it?"

"It's just better that way, okay?"

"Even the next day?"

"Even the next day."

"We'd be eaten alive out here."

"So what?" She looks out to a formation of granite jutting out over the water; up to the bright stars and moon shining through the final reaches of the atmosphere caught in the late sun. All of it goes as one. Take any part and take all of it. I look away. I think that to go there and sit through the night with her will strike at some core fantasy of mine. Something I should make real as evidence of a good life. Mom put it that way, and now I'm on the lookout for such moments everywhere. Things I can hold on to as a reminder to be grateful. I have many of these fantasies: like sitting at the controls of an airplane; or high on a mounting at night, a distant city winking behind the shadows of people who had come with me, all of us in the dark with the light of the city and the stars below us, at arms reach. Then again, what difference is there between dreams and memory? They are equally tangible in recollection. Equally valueless whenever it is I'm sat in bright room without any feature to it, forever. "Why did you say that at the Shouting Tree?" asks Lily. "Don't you know how much you embarrassed me?" She whirls to face me, and even though I'm ashamed to look at her, I do anyway. Resist how?

"I was trying to embarrass him," I say.

"But you embarrassed me."

"I know. I'm sorry."

She tilts her head a little, as she does. I feel like I'm under a microscope when she does it. Self-conscious of my own breathing, my own thoughts. "It's okay," she whispers.

Her breathless readiness to forgive a contention in my heart. An owl calls across the lake. I've gone off trail and onto the granite slab without thought, so backtrack to the trail and follow again.

We go on. Lily walks slower than I'd like and I faster than she'd like, so we settle on an in-between. "Maybe we can stay at Hakon's place?" she says.

"That's not a good idea."

"Why?"

"We're not so close." It's no lie, but it wouldn't be a problem for us to spend the night there. His mom would mend any argument between us with a big plate of fish sticks. It would be nothing to show up and ask to spend the night.

"I think we should. Or I could go there by myself," she says.

I walk faster and she falls ten, then twenty paces behind. The distance grows and I look back sometimes hoping to see her trying to catch up but she's content on the distance. I keep on until she's very small on the road, like a tiny inclusion of silver in a dark stone. She doesn't call out for me to stop and when there's a bend in the road I quickly disappear behind it.

From here I trekked into the woods and turned back to spy her through the trees, following parallel the trail for almost a mile that way. No need to do so now.

It's getting cold, and fast. A storm far to the east quakes with thunder. Turbulent eddies whip up the smell of pollen and sediment into the air. I move on down the trail. Soon, the quickening winds pulse through the trees in competing currents and an atmospheric melee begins, like the forward detachment of a ghost army meeting the vanguard of another. I go for shelter among the trees. Lightning strikes close, the bright filaments a thing I supply, for I've seen thousands. Sheets of electrical outbursts arcing over many miles of sky, sometimes extending beyond the storm into the clear night. The dark trees bow and sway. Most of them hold but some shed bulks of themselves that crash down through the canopy. The rain begins, large, articulate drops that say something of hail to come. A crack of thunder, curtains of rain lit fleetingly in the dark so vividly that I wonder from where it comes. The downpour tamps everything aground and the wind is cleaned of particulates. Hail is next – the size of sugar cubes. I hunker near the bole of a coniferous. The needles are torn from the brambles by the hail and they come down with the ice. I hold out my hands to catch some of the stones and eat them; much cleaner than the slime in my water pouch. A final throe of wind and hail and then the storm settles into a steady night-rain.

The land echoes with flood waters carving paths to lower planes and, ultimately, to Twin River. I gather more hailstones and eat them then stand with an idea to follow the rivulets, since they'll mask my footprints. But if I'm only going to the bridge spanning the river, what good would that do? If they've followed me to the trail, and if they know the land they'll know I have to cross the bridge anyway. Which means I need to hurry and beat them there.

I go, thrashing at the water-weighted limbs of the trees. The trail braids with many others to and from Slim Lake, so I stick to the woods running parallel to them all, finding my way by the feel of the ground and by some memorable facet that had struck me long ago. An old campsite tucked beside the shallow start of a mining prospect. Flaky remnants of coffee tins crunching hollowly underfoot. Bone-like protuberances of granite and more to involve the whole body, reading the tactile chronicle of the land like running a finger over a familiar line of braille. In a mile, the sound of rapids is unmistakable. The calm river is presently a great convection of flood waters. The bridge ahead groans against the force of it all. I hold just within the cover of woods and high grass before the approach.

She walks by, and waits at the abutment and looks back to scan the trees. I feel stupid, and wonder how embarrassing it might be to show myself and play it off as a joke. She has her hands in her pockets. There's nothing on her face but the effort of searching and then she turns and begins over the bridge.

The thunder is distant now, and the flares of lighting I can only hope are too far by now to light the bridge. The time for crossing has come, and I step out from the trees. The exposure felt like a phantom pressure in anticipation of pain or sudden nothingness, but neither come. I reach the abutment and start across Twin River Bridge.

<u>Sean</u>

The dead's father is sunworn to his bones. Years past the vanishing of his last youthful feature. His eyes are bright blue and wide with attentiveness but that dark rim around them is gone and the irises seem to bleed into the whites of them now. I offered him a photo of the body at first but he wanted to see it for himself, so we've come to the viewing room. I tell him I can wait outside but he insists I come with him. He's looking at the body through the glass when he says, "I don't know if I can tell you." In his broad hands he holds an old photo he brought of the dead man, of his son, the edges of it exaggerating an essential tremor in his hands. "It could be him, I suppose."

"Take all the time you need," I say.

He looks up at me like I've said something stupid. "I've taken the time, but you've got half his head covered up." He waves the picture at the body which has been only partially exposed – the face and neck and no more. I don't tell him that his ears are chewed off and we've got half his son's head covered up for his benefit. Instead, I say, "Is there anybody else who could ID him for sure?"

The man looks at the body in its pale and bloated condition and he shrugs again. I crane my head over to spy the photo he's got. The son had gained considerable weight before he was killed, and the bloat doesn't help, but it's him. "What happens if I can't ID the body?" he asks.

"We can do a DNA test to determine kinship."

"And if I refuse that?"

"There's no rush, sir. Take all the time you need."

"I've taken the time, just answer my question." His hands are trembling even more now.

"Well sir, you waive your right to claim the remains, then after a time we dispose of the body."

He contemplates the photo and the body again. "And if I identify it?"

"We move on with the investigation, elevated to homicide." This is true whether or not he identifies the body, but I hope putting in in such a way will convince him to do it now so we can better commit ourselves to finding the bastards responsible.

"Is that what you think this is?" He asks. His wide and pale-blue eyes are looking through me, through the walls of the room.

"I do, sir."

"Does that mean you'll stop searching for him?"

I look down at my feet to hide any tell of impatience then back at the man. "Yes sir, it does."

"Then why would I claim a body you've offered up to me half by hearsay?"

"Whose hearsay?"

"Yours, sir." He looks at me square now, his whole body given to the act like he means to start something.

"If there's anyone else-"

"There's no one else. Brother died of a heart attack five years ago. Mother admitted for as long and neither have I seen the man you want me to identify in that time." He takes his cap off and beats it against his thigh and puts it back on again. Grass spikelets drift to the tile floor.

"Sir, we've got nothing else to go on about your missing son. There's nowhere else to look and we've got other missing people tying up manpower."

"Those people go missing before or after my son?"

I breathe. The body through the glass does itself no favors at all, made almost anonymous with bloat. But when I look back the old man is crying. The tremor in his hands spreads to his whole body and he goes to the wall and leans on it and crumples like a bellows with each sob. I go to the opposite wall and stare down at the floor. Give him space. Silence. He gathers himself with a few stuttering breaths, then he says, "Okay, alright."

"Is he your son, sir?"

"He is."

"Okay"

Back at the station I find McLloyd in his office scowling over paperwork. "Webb," he says without looking when I enter.

"I wanted to update you. The father ID'd my guy. He..."

Aaron's phone is buzzing but he doesn't seem to care. His pen lashes the signature line of a document then he puts it in a folder and produces another from the same and scans it rapidly. "And what?"

"You're busy," I say, backtracking through the door.

"Sean."

"Sir?"

"Tell me." He still doesn't look up at me.

"It's nothing."

"Nothing? No questions for the father?"

"The father hasn't seen his son in five years."

"Do I have to order an interview?"

"I'm telling you, he knows nothing. The entire family is estranged. He could hardly ID the body at all."

"What about his friends, coworkers? Christ, Webb what the hell is the matter with you?"

"Look, we both know this was a random murder,

like all the others. Nobody who the victim knew is the killer. The crumbs end where they begin at the disappearance of Avery," I say.

His eyes flash to mine, then return as fast to his paperwork. He situates himself upright then clears his throat of nothing and says, "You want me to leave it up to your hunch?"

"Of course not, sir."

"Then I want a list of names with any relationship to the dead man on my desk by the end of the day." He makes a motion with his hand for me to leave, and I do.

Was I looking for a reaction? A part of me was.

I pass through the cellular columns of desks on the main level. The place is entirely too big for its use to us. We occupy maybe a fourth of the space available, and what's true here is true of Ely entirely. The hospitals, shopping malls, and home developments are too large and too numerous. The population of Ely was expected to expand, but the opposite happened. A shame perhaps, but on second thought, would it have been good for the city to have grown to fill the walls of its police stations, its hospitals and mortuaries?

At the other end of the floor the receptionist comes through the glass doors. By her haste she has something important to pass on, and she means to tell Aaron first. I move to intercept her. "Something the matter?" I ask. She stops, looking to Aaron's office then back at me.

"Jessica Albane is here and wants a word with Chief McLloyd," she says. "He wasn't answering."

"The Chief is busy. She mention what for?" I gesture the way she'd come and we begin back through the door and down the stairs to reception.

"She wouldn't say."

We come into the foyer and the girl is there wrapped up in a crochet sweater and a scarf and clutching a stack of photographs in her hand. It's clear on her face she's no real hope of achieving anything here; her eyes and manner conveying no amount of incredulity when she sees me. "Ms Albane?" She nods. I tell her the Chief is tied up at the moment, but I'd be glad to pass anything along to him. She nods again and I show her to the interview room more appropriate for non-suspects, furnished with artificial plants and a bureau drawer with nothing in it and some paintings and a wooden coffee table flanked by comfortable lawsons. She sits in the chair facing the oaken door, clutching the stack of photographs like warding charms. "Are those for us?" She nods and brings them away from her chest then holds them out for me. Some difficulty parting with them. I take them and sit.

In the stack are pictures of fallen birch trees and a funnel web hidden in the cone of a broken tree limb. Pictures of bugs, birds, strange rocks and the remnants of an old campsite with rusted tins and ironware the color of the clay they're strewn. Pictures of red squirrels and chipmunks nibbling peanut butter from their paws. His green cabin, a woman in the window, motion blurred like the rain streaked in the foreground. Another of the neighboring cabin just after sun down. A gothic subject.

"They're William's," she says. "I found them with his old things and figured they" – she breathes – "figured they'd help to find where he could be going."

"What do you mean, where he *could* be going?"

"Is communication slow at ECPD? I've explained this to your Chief," she says.

"Explain it to me, if it's no trouble."

She tells me that William has photographic memory – didn't use the phrase exactly, but describes as much. What follows is a kind of eulogy, and I'll sum the facts of it and no more. She says William used to take Moxie out and travel miles of trails and dirt roads and the deep woods with nothing to navigate with but memory. She tells me she'd been skeptical until witnessing him in places that he'd seen before. In those places, she says he seemed to lead Moxie more than the other way, and that often he respected the boundaries of things not there, and when she asked him what they were, he'd tell her in such detail and conviction that he'd have to be a psychopath to be making it all up. She goes still and quiet as if to reckon with that possibility, and then she tells me of a sketch she found of the suspect of those killings long ago. She has it on her phone and holds it up. Says it bears resemblance to William, her voice wavering on the edge of breaking down. I tell her such drawings are unreliable.

In the stack is a picture of a wan sun over the water. Pictures of trees grown into themselves and their neighbors like the grafted bone of a vanished twin. A picture of an owl peering frightfully down at the cyclopean thing capturing it. Clouds like waves on the open ocean. The night, poorly lit, the moon blurred and the dark twist of tree limbs enshadowed by it. People. Children at camp. Oh god. "This is good. Thank you," I say.

"Will they help?"

"Yes, I think so. I'll pass them around, see if anyone recognizes something."

I doubt it's what she wants to hear, but she nods anyway. There's more she wants to say, that much is clear, and now she's rubbing her hands together without the photographs to occupy them. "I read it was Aaron's brother and his family killed," she says. "Is that true?"

"It is."

She nods and looks down at her hands locked tightly in themselves. "This must be very personal for him." Then she shakes her head. "I'm sorry. It's not like that at all."

"Aaron doesn't think it's the same people responsible," I tell her. "He believes these are copycat killings. A symptom of Ely's decline."

She looks at me. "But what do you think?" Her previous disposition of quiet impatience is gone in that instant. All the tells of it stilled, the tension and uncertainty of her hands, her wandering eyes, things like that. She would wait here a very long time for my answer, it seems.

"We missed something then," I say. "I believe finding William alive is somehow the same as finding out what that was."

She breathes, stands and looks around at the ersatz things in the interview room, things made to be lighter and cheaper than the authentic objects they stand in for as though to be whisked away like stage props upon her departure. How do I reassure her? Of what? There's nothing.

She walks to the door and I see her from the building. Our footfalls echo in the foyer, empty but for the brass statue at the base of the stairs of our most beloved Police Chief many decades ago: a regal doberman named Hal. It was transferred here from the old police building and looks out of place among the modern cut-rate.

Jessica leaves out the tall oak doors and into the parking lot, too tired for farewells. It's raining outside. A sunshower to stand a long time in, but the photos in my hand are getting wet. Fragile truths are often stitched together from such tatters as these, and I tuck them safely under my arm and return inside.

Gibbs is hunched at his computer screen, blue-lit in the dim and vast room. There are five others here and I gather them at Gibbs' desk. "Pay close attention everyone. Each of these is a lead," I say in a low voice, holding the stack of Polaroids in the air. "Each of these is someplace William has been; somebody he knew. Corporeal captures of the man's memory, which happens to be as good. You understand?"

"He's blind," observes Gibbs. "If he's going anywhere it's not on purpose."

"Nevermind that then. I want you to find where these were taken, and who's in them. Camp records, school records, residential. Everything. I want a map drawn up with points of interest and every possible destination marked on it in three hours. Here, ten photos each. Who's first?"

They take their shares and go to work. I've selected some photographs for myself and step into my office and begin. Various residences. William's cabin. The neighbor's and a few unknown homes like one of a one-story cabin with a triangular dormer window; firelight making shadows on the ceiling. Another looks like a boathouse, everything enshadowed against the still water but for the window and the open front door both lit up by interior lights. Through the door is a yellowed love-seat, pink flowers and curling green stems. There is no address.

I search the police blotter first for records of the McLloyd residence: 14755 N. Pineshire Wy. But the cabin in the Polaroid is different from the one on screen. Surely, he would have gone there. He would have known Lily. They went to camp together. They're pictured standing side-by-side in one of the photographs. I search for it in my stack and study it awhile. On the computer I bring up yearbook photos from Fox Elementary and Owl Middle School. Lily McLloyd, smiling in her 8th grade photo. It's definitely her, in the picture.

There's a knock at my door. "Cap, I have something here," says Gibbs through it. I step out. "Seems William was buds with some Norwegian immigrant named Hakon Halvosen. 12539 N Flint Rd." He shows me a picture of the residence on the screen of a laptop held in his hands. It matches the one pictured in one of the Polaroids. "Get me a map, nothing newer than o-eight." I say to the others.

"Ahead of you," says Gibbs and we go to his desk. "Five miles North of Slim Lake."

"He can't have made it that far yet. We have time to get there before him. Get a heli above the area and Calvary to those coordinates. Tell them armed and dangerous are likely in tow of William."

"Aye," says Gibbs, and I start toward the stairwell. "Where you going?" he asks.

"With the greeting party."

William

Over the flooded river is thunder, a final dull rumble before everything is muted behind the hiss of the rapids. The water spills over the deck of the bridge and froths between the boards, and the rail vibrates on its spindles. I inch along, gripping the rail made smooth by the contributing abrasions of many others who did likewise. The entire structure rocks like a diesel generator. My own weight is meaningless against the force of the river below. Near the crest I let go from the rail and move left to right, carving as arbitrary a path as I can on the narrow way, to make for a more difficult target. At the crest of the bridge the deck sags steeply into the water. A pier has likely given out and the floods now rush energetically over the boards. I cling to the balustrade where the deck is lifted up from the pressure of the torrents, but is still shallowly drowned under the racing water. I step into it. My boots hold against the rapids for all of a second, and then my feet slide from the deck and the power of the river threatens to rip me from the bridge, but instead, I'm pressed against one of the pickets. I struggle back to my feet then scoot across the drowned area. Drenched and cold but no worse off, I resume the right to left serpentine over the last span of the bridge. Before reaching the end of it I run instead into the canopy of an uprooted tree draped over the deck, the bough pressed against the left side rail. There's no way around it, so I push through, loud enough to hear over the river. Should I turn back? Turn back where? You've come too far for that.

I press on, and when I emerge from the branches I veer immediately left in search of the handrail again, groping for it, grasping in the air, when over the sounds of rushing water, someone calls from the woods. I don't hear what, or rather, I don't process the words. What I do instead is freeze, totally still, but only for a second. I've heard a call like that before and I know it's a common tactic a hunter might use to still their quarry for a better shot. I'm not so easily fooled, and I dash to the ground right as the shot rings out. But the bullet is too quick, and it finds my clavicle anyway. I hit the ground. There's no pain at first, just a pressure and a warmth, but soon the nerves find the small hole occupying my trapezes and then it's like barbed-wire has been sown through my flesh. They were waiting for me. God, I was too long getting here.

Their voices leap out from over the sounds of the rapids, muffled and triumphant. Boots rapping now over the wooden deck. Two sets of them at least. They'll come to stand over and mock me. They'll make it more personal than that. A brief torture; especially the case if I succeeded in killing their bloodhound. Maybe they'll notice that I'm blind and could never identify them for police, but it won't matter. By now, I'm just another victim of theirs.

I've a special contempt for dying like that – more than the usual fear of it I suppose – and a molten rage leaps into my heart. With sudden effort, I roll off the edge of the bridge and into the flooded river; into the cold. The currents sweep me away and take me under. When I break above the water the men are shouting and one of them fires into the river, the buckshot splashing down near. I'm pulled under again. Cold seeps into my bones and saps my will to fight. I'm going numb, and any sense for what's up or what's down is then inferred by vestibular diligence alone, but even that becomes lost and then there's only a sense of tumbling and crashing through the gripping cold. By chance I'm spat out above the water, gasping, then taken under once more. I'll drown very soon, the warmth of my body averaged out over the miles of Twin River, recycled back into the land.

A bright light and a bright pain. There then gone. It was a boulder cutting up from the riverbed. Unavoidable. Saw it before it happened it seemed, like waking from sleep and fumbling the order of occurrence to believe I dreamed of what woke me before it could have. The light is brighter than it's ever been.

Drifting in a shallow lake bed now. The sun enfolded

spectacularly in the ripples and waves. Elodea grasps at my legs, their stems going down a depth I cannot see and I swim to the bright sun and burst through the surface and take in iron-rich water instead of air.

Anti-anesthetic, this. Lucid again, I reach into the whipping waters for anything at all and brush the slippery stones of the riverbed, then I twist around and swim opposite them only to be turned around and around again. An idea to go limp bargains with the desire to fight the currents, and I spread out flat, arms out like a skydiver fording gale-force winds and I emerge face down above the water and flip over and take in the air. With my legs pointed down stream and arms wading I'm able to keep my head above the water. There's now a dilating iris of light pulsing with the heart, a terrible aching at the center of my thoughts. The rapids are too violent for me to latch onto anything near the banks. I have no choice but to ride it out to calmer waters, and I drift for a long time in the braided currents until they change, going vertical and fanning out wide and spinning me on the surface like a fallen leaf. Calm now. The shadow of pine and vaulting rock sculptures pass against the stars. From where? Unknown. From nowhere.

With my ears underwater, everything sounds equidistant. The miles of river are brought to me like a sound in the night from a distant window opened to the quiet darkness. Fear that all places would expand into an infinity, sound having little capacity to define the limits of things in an open place. Fear of being spun around and lost with no way to recover my place in it all. I lift my ears above the water to listen for rapids ahead but there's only the opened channel now, conveying many tonnes of water and debris silently in the pitch of night and beyond my inner maps, onto territories traveled once or two times or never traveled at all. I'm pulled along that dark scrawl of the river for some time. How fast am I going? Hard to tell, but sometimes there's the sound currents curling around a tree that had fallen into it or around a sharp turn, and near these I can tell that the river flows no more than five miles an hour.

I enter a patch of wooden particulates captured in a slow kolk and roll over and over in the water, trading the strength gone from my arms for that left in my back and core, and soon I run aground, numbly dragged over the rocks until I'm able to grab hold of something beneath the water – wedged tree limb – and I pull myself against the current and onto the bank. I crawl a distance from the water like something will pluck me from the bank and throw me back in, then I lie in the silt with the smell of moss and iron and cinnamon coming off it. Strange thoughts orbit the edges of consciousness no wakeful mind would conjure up. I'm aware of their dreamlike quality in brief grasps but am no more in control: The last plane ride out of here. A deer on the runway holding up takeoff. Myself at the window seat. "Stop holding my hand," I say. Mom lets go. Takeoff. There's little to see beyond the green-white light. The land rolls by like a series of crude maps fed onto a conveyor belt.

They'll follow the river. I need to go. Only, there is no going. I'm dreaming. Even still, it suits me to imagine that I do stand and walk into the cover of the woods. A dark woods against a bright sky, the canopies creating the pattern of wings as if a thousand glass moths took flight as one. With every step the forest grows, or perhaps, I shrink away. This, in some relation to the distance traveled, and soon I'm not traveling at all. Every stride takes me no further than that of an insect. I step off a short ledge and land on termite-brittle wood like I've plunged my hands into packing peanuts. Certainly I'm moving, my legs ache with the effort.

The horizon is a blossom of windows glowing with TV static. The horizon is a blossom of eyes, wings, of hair and all the spaces between the trees make the negatives of people standing at strange angles – her neck is craned unnaturally, offset from the contortion of her shoulders under the blanket. People sick in the head hold themselves differently. By some law it's like they have to embody their sickness somehow. She;s lived a long time undergoing a transformation and now she's haphazard, all gaunt and stringy, her flesh slapped onto her bones like clay onto a wire-figurine and never brought properly to form.

I've walked Lily home many times before, and each time she insisted that we part before getting too close. I took her reluctance as diligence on the part of her parents against boys who would take advantage of her. This time she walked me right up to the front door, and now I know that's not it at all.

It's an old home, but in no worse shape than my

own. A two-story with an attic and a round window and two pillars under the gable.

Lily says, "goodbye," and then she opens the door and leaves it open for me to watch her go up the stairs on the other end of the living room. The woman is sitting on the sofa in a nest of downy blankets with the spines of the feathers poking out from the worn seams. Her head tracks Lily across the room and up the stairs and when she's gone the woman looks at me and tells me to shut the door.

The following Sunday, Lily brings me right to the door of her home again and goes up the stairs just as before. Where to? She doesn't speak to her mother this time either, and the woman hasn't moved from the sofa. She's smoking a cigarette. There's an ashtray full of them burnt down to their cotton filters. Flakes of ash dusting the coffee table. I muster the courage to step through the doorway and wave, politely. I tell her my name but she only looks on. A man speaks from another room inside and the woman on the couch says to him, "Oh, don't you bother. You stay upstairs." In her voice is that feminine mocking to pick at your bones. He says something back and in return the woman says, "You fell asleep." She lights another cigarette, the glint of the flame shining in her dark eyes. She's looking at me. "What if it's an animal, or a crazy person breaking in and you're asleep up there?"

This gets nothing from the man, so she says, "You should know that I spoke with your brother about this. He told me it isn't the first time you let something like that happen."

"You don't know what you're talking about," says the man, audible at last.

"Sure I do. He said back then your radio wasn't shot out at all, and that you fell asleep!" There's no smile on her face to match it in her voice.

"He doesn't know shit, either."

I want to leave but I don't.

The place smells of days old dinner left out on plates; of cigarettes and stagnation. There's an old bird cage stood near the television, droppings on the floor and loose feathers too, but there's no bird inside. The woman looks so tired. Her eyes are all swallowed up by the folds of her lids like ball magnets thrown into iron clay.

Do I remember that right? Did I think of it then how I do now? There's nothing near to tell. I'm not there. I'm concussed and hallucinating.

"You fell asleep," she says again, her mouth pinned up into a smile now. A shame for her resemblance to Lily. The man thunders down the stairs and onto the landing – a small and swarthy man not much taller than me – and he turns and lifts his shirt to reveal a knot of shiny skin on his shoulder, around which the muscles are atrophied. "What's this then?" He asks. There's a performative nature to it. It's like I'm being shown on purpose. I recognize the ritual from my own parents when they almost split. When things get bad people compete for the favorable judgment of others, even children, in preparation for the big fight. I guess it's so everyone knows which side to take in the aftermath. "What about this?" he says, revealing lacerations on his lower back.

The woman laughs.

The horizon is a blossom of teeth and facets of the moon. My feet drag through knee-deep water and a reflected counterpart develops to it all, like a moving Rorschach.

Sean

We're going seventy down the highway with the wind cutting through the cracked weatherstripping of my door. A line of eighteen-wheelers make way ahead of us and we scream past with the siren bouncing off their hulls. A helicopter goes over, the beating of its blades vibrating the window glass. Its red strobe light on the tail stitches across the black sky and our own lights lash the woods in brief red and blue glimpses. The helicopter ignites its searchlight and the dark below takes form: pine spires shooting high into the air, and deep in the woods the charred remains of a cabin is immolated in the light. Jefferson one-hands the bottom of the steering wheel as he turns us onto a neglected road with the pavement cracked then spalled, then gone. He stops the cruiser a ways from the blackened cabin and two accompanying cars pull up on our flanks, angling their headlights and spotlights to illuminate one-hundred-eighty degrees of darkness around us. I climb from the cruiser with my sig-sauer drawn. "Shouldn't we wait for more?" says Jefferson. He's got a shotgun casually rested over his protruding belly.

"We're enough. Eyes out," I say, and radio my intent to approach the cabin. We set up in a loose formation. The helicopter's downdraft rustles the tops of the trees, frightening birds from their roosts that catch the light as they fling themselves from danger in a bright blur. I turn the light on under the nose of my pistol and shine it into any shadow deep and large enough to conceal a man. The flanking officers sweep out and we approach as one.

The crozzled scales of the cabin shine under the halide of the helicopter like a subject under interrogation, revealing nothing. We surround the building with someone posted at each corner while I step within the beams bearing only themselves. The roof is gone. Signs of human habitation here and there. Sleeping arrangements and empty cans of food and artifacts important only to drifters: wirespool and tools and other scavenged things, as if gathered by a sutler to an army of addicts. Yet everything is caked with too much muck to have been touched or trod recently. On the windowsill are picture frames, the glass shattered and the photos gone to white or always were. The bathroom seems to have been spared from the flames, but there's nothing to find in there and I leave out the front door. "Avian One, strafe the southern road. We've arrived before them," I say into the radio. The pilot affirms and the helicopter angles off, its searchlight proceeding meticulously through the trees along the road. The other officers gather around me with their weapons and mounted lights held at their black boots. "We'll search the neighboring homes. One at a time," I tell them. There are two: one to the north and another south. We hit the latter first and find it toppled into itself like matchsticks balanced into the make of a home then set afire. At the center of it all is a pale object reflecting our lights back at us. I climb half through the ruin before realizing that it's a porcelain toilet dragged there. Like a prank to mock a most essential instinct. The paleness of it sanding out in the dark and in the gnarled woodwork. Come, look closer, and now squint. Fool. What did you think it would be? A nymph? The thing you were looking for?

Who did all this? All of it here in this city and everywhere? The Devil is a jester. The Devil an abandoned son.

We move on to the northern home. It's intact and boarded up tight, but the front door has been breached. Inside, the plaster of the interior walls is crumbled to the floor. It looks purposeful. In the beams are exposed screws worn to rusty and twisted nubs and there's a pentagram spray-painted on the floor of the living room. Beer bottles strewn everywhere. I holster my pistol. There's no one here.

Through my radio comes the pilot of Avian One: "Twin River flows over the bridge. Doubt we'll find anyone come south of it."

"Search the banks," I say. The blades hack at the air at high deflection and the chopper turns sharp to the west. Backup arrives then. A dozen SAR personnel, each with their own idea of haste, climbing from their vehicles and federating out in preparation to move wherever it is we pick up a fresh trail. But there won't be one. This was a wasted effort. William never made it this far.

Another helicopter swings out in a wide arc, and every new arrival is a mark against any future effort of mine. I direct it south anyway, to comb the trails and roads leading here. Jefferson finds me on the patio of the boarded-up home and asks, "What do we do now?" while delousing his glasses on his shirt sleeve.

"We go to Flint Bridge, south of here."

He and I take the cruiser there. The thunder of the floods comes through the glass. Jefferson shuts the headlights off and we idle in a patch of high grass some paces from the road, peering out the windows with our guns clutched up under our chins. Satisfied there's no ambush awaiting us, I climb out and go first to an old wood chipper rotting on the fringe of the road with the smell of bad oil coming off it. I shine the light into the feed. Expecting what? Inside are foxes, their eyes shining back. Behind them are the metal feed rollers. One of the gray kits comes into the light as if to mistake it for day, waddling and cooing softly. The mother cries out at me.

We move on, keeping off the road to avoid ruining any prints that might be there, and we go to the river where the flood rapids arc over unseen prominences in the bed. An immense force behind it all. The middle of the bridge is drowned and the whole thing barely keeps to form. I squat down and pan my light over the road and into the trees lining the sides and over the approach, where there are the unmistakable pattern of shadows made by the slight indentations of prints. I whistle. Jefferson turns, and his own light limns me near the bridge. "What?" he says.

"Stop pointing that thing at me and come over here," I tell him.

He does and squats down. "What is it?"

"You don't see them?"

"I don't see shit. Why are we alone?"

I head over to the bridge, going slow, looking out for any tamped or broken stems in the tall grass but there's nothing like that. But leading to the bridge is the scattering of prints and of bike tracks, thought there are no dog prints anywhere. "Call it in," I say all the same.

"Call what in?"

"Have I lost it, or are those fresh tracks?"

He calls them in while I go to the sharp cut of the river. There's a warmth or energy to the air here. Like something has or is about to happen. They got him here and threw him in the river, didn't they? Which means that by some conspiracy of events Aaron was right all this time. Twin River runs eventually to Burntside Lake. William's body should turn up there in the next day or so.

"Hay Cap," says Jefferson. "Chief orders us back."

"Us?"

"Everybody."

"Tell him we've picked up a trail and we're not going anywhere."

There are no prints going east with the flow of

the river, and neither do any go west against it. They know we're following them and they know not to take any obvious paths that would make spotting their prints easy. I want to cross the bridge and get a look at the other side but it's a risk with the water going over and the structure rattling like it'll give any second.

"How do we know it's them?" asks Jefferson. A question relayed to me, no doubt.

"How do we know anything is?"

Jefferson mumbles some version of that through the radio, then he tells me, "Chief wants everyone at Burntside. He says you can stay, though."

I turn and take Jefferson's radio right from his hands. "Bring a goddamn canine unit to Flint Bridge. Over." I hand the radio back and the man looks slighted, but I don't give a damn.

When the canine unit arrives he sits in his truck awhile then lets the bloodhound out from the back and harnesses it then brings the dog over the tracks a few times and into the surrounding woods. The hound only takes him in circles. It's a closed loop. The man shakes his head at me and says, "With the wind and rain he can't get shit, man."

The moon peaks through a break in the clouds, momentarily illuminating the river in its torsional stampede into darkness. Whatever energy there was in this place is dissipating, becoming inert while I stand here. It's a crime scene and we're abandoning it.

Jefferson watches me, and he taps the mic of his radio against his side impatiently, like he has someplace better to be. We climb into the cruiser and travel some thirty minutes back to the Station, all that time in silence.

There, Gibbs is still parsing through the photos I gave him. "Anything?" I ask.

"Most of it's just trees and other bullshit," he says. "Chief wants a word with you."

"I'm sure he does. He'll probably bench me."

"I heard it all over the radio, but I don't think he'll bench you." Gibbs shakes his head with his lips in a doubtful frown. "He'll just tear into ya. His way. He'd run out of men quick suspending everybody over any mistake." From his lapel pocket he takes out a small flask and drinks.

"Don't push your luck."

"But who else will look through these photographs?" He chuckles and drinks again.

It wasn't just any mistake. I ignored Aaron's instructions then sent half the department on a goose chase. He'll bench me for sure.

I go into Aaron's office. The both of us are silent for as long as it takes us to measure how angry the other is in comparison to ourselves. "It's about now I suspect obstruction," I say. Aaron began with something about rank, but now he's looking at me like I've drawn a weapon on him.

"Captain, I've got forty square miles of rocks and leaves to turn over looking for these guys. I don't need subordinates tying up the entire department going every damn place William photographed once."

"They were there. I was there. We've got an

exposed crime scene at Flint Bridge that'll be swept away under your nose."

"You found some prints on a footbridge and you've come to the notion it's a crime scene?"

"Who else would be prodding around in a thunderstorm at night?" I say, but it's in my voice. A lack of conviction. If I sense it, so does he. Aaron scoffs like it's the most ridiculous thing he's ever heard. I go on: "You won't even consider that he's gone north. That he's going to your brother's."

"What would he go there for?" he asks, but I don't answer. He's too confident and doesn't appear concerned at all. Only amused. An act? Maybe. "Answer me," he says. But I'm upset. Too emotional. I can't have this conversation without preparation. If there's more to this, then I suspect Aaron has practiced all his life for this moment, and here I am stumbling into it like an idiot. "Speak your mind," he demands.

"Forget it."

"I don't think I will. Tell me what you're accusing me of."

"We don't have the time." I turn to leave.

"You go through that door without answering me and I'll suspend you to the conclusion of this manhunt, understand?"

Yes, I've no doubt he's iterated through a confrontation just like this one a hundred times in his head. A thousand times.

I turn to him. "You know, I've ridden sideseat for years, Aaron. Antagonistically so, oftentimes. Maybe it's just now caught up to me. Or maybe there's more."

"Well?"

"I've got nothing."

"You accuse me of obstruction with nothing?"

"That's right, sir."

"Then you're removed. Use your free time to gather your wits." He shuffles the papers on his desk meaninglessly, then, seeing I've not moved, he studies me. I give him a look that I hope conveys neither defiance nor surrender, then leave.

My thoughts are inchoate. Hardly there at all, and he forced them out that way before I understood them myself. He forced nothing. You were emotional. Stupid! Then again, he made a mistake too, benching me. Gather my wits indeed.

I head to Case Records at once.

The lights of the basement are off and I keep them that way, holding the beam of my flashlight low to the yellowed carpet. At the end of the room on a gray metal door, "Records" is stenciled in black arial. There's a red band of light over the electronic keypad. The code was never changed from factory default: one through six. I punch it in and the pad chirps success tones and the magnetic lock slides from the frame and I open the door and flip the lights on to a room in disarray. Accordions of files slumped at the base of full cabinets and tote boxes. It seems after a while everybody started tossing the files anywhere they pleased. It's all recorded electronically, and it would definitely be easier to go through them that way, but handling the physical copies inspires deeper focus, I find.

The oldest records should be filed in the

cabinets so I start there, the bottom drawer. The manila folders are tabbed by the decade. Nineteen-seventy seem like a good place to start, and I slide the folder out and undo the brass fastener and begin. The decade was typical for the time. Some domestic disturbances. The body of an old woman turned up in Twin River, assumed to have drowned, for a suspicious wound to the side of her head. It was deemed accidental anyway. Several addenda were added to the file more than a decade later reexamining that determination. But even with new insights given to police by more recent events her death was never updated to homicide. She was certainly alive when she received the blow to the back of her head, but it could have occurred when she had fallen into the river.

The first confirmed murder occurred in eighty-nine. A sixty-five year-old trucker was found dead inside his eighteen-wheeler with twelve gunshot wounds into his side. Someone emptied a clip of forty-five through the door and just walked away. Exploratory. Possibly testing the waters to find that Ely City Police were not ready for things to come. The case went cold after just a month. Interviews of local residents were a lackadaisical effort. Three in all: the wife of the deceased; another of a gas-station tenant on Highway One; and the last of a man who said he'd heard shots from his porch at five AM.

"Jeremy Gills claims he heard a "pop-pop, pop-pop" sound from his residence a mile east of the crime scene. No further details were obtained." Stunning work. Maybe they thought the killer would move on if they played dead? Seven years later another murder occurred in the area. This one a departure from the previous. Cooper Walt, a man in his fifties, was found dead with a hundred and six shallow stab wounds about the neck and face near the eastern shore of Burntside Lake. A final coup de gras from a twenty-two longrifle in the back of his head. The perpetrator was then given the appellation, "Weakling Killer" by the newspapers, since everything about the crime suggesting it was carried out by a particularly feeble person. Some old or disabled man, a small woman, or a pre-teen. All were considered, none were ascertained. This time the investigation was more earnest with Aaron at the helm of homicide. Fifteen interviews of any residence with a view of the waters where the dead was last seen in his fishing boat.

An hour pouring over these interviews. The consensus: while Cooper was drag-fishing he was coaxed ashore somehow and led to the scene of his demise. One interviewee claimed he saw a small figure walking into the woods behind the man from his own dock. "He moved like a kid. Carried himself like the world was still under him, you know? I thought nothing strange about it except that it was Cooper, who wasn't fond at all of children." Astonishingly, the interviewing detective failed to ask him why that was, and if there were kids in the neighborhood he had problems with? From the man's testimony a facial composite was derived, the very one Ms. Albane found off the web. Laughable in its generality, but certainly a young boy.

All of the stab wounds were non-fatal and inflicted before the killshot. It's inconceivable a grown man, fifty or otherwise, would allow some kid to do that to them without putting up a fight. What's more, if it was just a kid it means the murder of eighty-nine is unrelated.

I read on.

Three years later is the double homicide of a young couple camping in an area just west of Slim Lake. The killer had cut open their tent with a knife and shot the man in the head while he slept. The poor girl was put to the blade. Again, shallow wounds, though some were enough to kill this time, and there was no need to finish the victim off with the firearm.

Signs of a struggle, or of another's presence? None at all. There was hardly any struggle. Hard to believe if the victim thought she had a chance to overpower her attacker. Then again maybe the victim was the kind to go limp and dull in the head? There's evidence she'd been led around like an animal, like the killer was amused that the girl had evidently entered a state of obedient catatonia. I wonder if she thought it would save her?

I move on.

Multiple disappearances between the second and last of the known murders, appended to the Weakling Killings merely by their proximity and timing. The last of the confirmed killings occurs in ninety-nine. A triple homicide, and the final escalation. An old and lonely trucker was the first victim. Second, a community-known fisherman. Then a young couple taking their first breaths of marriage. And last, a family, butchered while camping on the shores of Burntside.

A Beacon in the Light

The father, Daniel McLloyd, the mother Emily and their twelve year old daughter Lily, all of them bore wounds deep and precise from practice. Lily received the least brutality of the three, stabbed only once in the chest. She looks alive in the photo of her, partially interred in the leaves. Her pale neck and her tawny hair neat around her face, and her mouth and eyes closed and arms folded in front as though to receive the last vestige of mercy yet abandoned wholesale in the mind of her murderer. Lily might have been special to the killer. Known to him. Ultimately, whatever reluctance or regret the killer might have had for harming her meant nothing. Her suffering was greater for it. The wound in her chest was barely fatal, slightly nicking the circumflex artery of her fragile heart. A centimeter shallower and she would be here to tell what had transpired.

I'm suddenly aware of my own heart, of its fluttering and fragility, like a separate thing the body is built around to keep safe.

The mother and father were given no considerations. Their bodies so disfigured as to become anonymous. Wounds about the arms and hands indicate they had fought, but their efforts preserved nothing of the killer. Neither of them had so much as dragged their nails over the assailants skin for later finding. No tufts of hair yanked from the follicle or blood spilled but their own. Notably, the bodies were three days old when found, but a witness described Daniel's truck driving in the backwoods a day before discovery. Also notable was the lack of essential camping supplies. They brought with them a single tent and sausages to cook but no means to cook them; no dishware or utensils, pots pans nor a stove. They were certainly moved there. But this is a departure from the usual methodology. The killer, or killers, had never moved any bodies before. Likely this was an effort to afford the killer time to sterilize the true location of the crime scene. But why?

Avery Compton.

A page is dedicated to him as sole witness. He'd been found a mile south of the supposed scene of the murders, heat-exhausted and four days missing, sitting on a picnic table with his head down and unresponsive. In that state he was taken to the hospital, dehydrated and fevered. It took two days before he was able to speak and he did so first with his father Henry, who would not allow police to question his son. When they got a judge to order an interview of Avery he claimed he had trouble remembering what happened, and got his doctor to explain that he suffered blindness in one eye and partial in the other. This, and with his delirium upon discovery, any testimony of his was therefore subject to doubt. Notably, Avery never attempted to claim he had merely stumbled on the bodies near Burntside.

I toss the documents from my lap onto the parsed pile of them near the door. I believe Avery saw what happened. And if it's true he can go place to place with memory alone then his testimony is to be believed. He's working through what he remembers now, if alive. He could be alive. Touch the framework of a spider's web and it shoots off to safety in a blur, over a pattern of support threads woven within a maze of capture threads. It does this by the same process William navigates by his own inner cartography that must take him, among many places, to the true location of the McLloyd murders.

William

There's deadwood floating in the chest-high water. Bitter cold. The pool spins counterclockwise from a current feeding in from the flooded river. I want to warm myself but how?

He makes a circle for the fire next to a cedar tree far enough from its canopy so not to melt the snow from the branches. He tells me to fetch kindling and I march around and gather twigs and pine needles and pile them into a little tipi in the fire circle. "Strike a flame to it," he says, but my fingers are too stiff. He watches as I warm them on my neck before striking a match onto the kindling. The flames crack and burst out from the duff like escaped things. We gather more wood before the sun goes down. The moon is full and we can see for miles over the slopes of blue snow and the black shards that are trees. So clear and bright it brings into doubt my account of it. We sit by the fire for a long time in silence. After a while I ask him, "Will you end up separated?"

He looks at the flames a long time. "I don't know. It's just, we're afraid."

"Of what?"

"Your mom is scared of what might happen if we stay. I'm scared of what might happen if we leave."

"You mean what might happen to me."

A steady plum of steam rolls out from his mouth. "I already told you it's not your fault."

"I know it's not."

He looks at me and shakes his head. "No you don't."

My hands are numbed to insensitive clubs. I need to dry them but my clothes are wet, so I just beat them against my sides to get the blood going. An immense pain gathers in my shoulder doing this. Shot there... right.

The air sits still like the cold has gripped it with everything else. Crystalline sculptures dress the branches of naked trees like tinsel. All the animals are arrested to their dens and the lakes are frozen over too. Nothing moves but us, and we stop sometimes in the woods listening to the miniature symbols chime when the shadows move and the sun breaks the tiny ice crystals that grow in the night or shade. So small a sound as to confuse its origin, acting on a part of the ear that captures the workings of the body, the heart, the spine and shoulders ratcheting a little. It's cold enough to snow but it hasn't yet and it won't today. There are no clouds but for those that are like feathers high enough to catch the light of the sun long before it's risen and long after it's set. Everything is on the verge of change; becoming frozen, made still, numb and pale. We don't talk. There's only so much to say before the scripts go dull from repeat. The lines and the places they were spoken coming to mind and discouraging any attempt at rehashing. I've learned that silence is okay sometimes.

We come to a frozen stream under a glulam footbridge. There's a narrow avenue of flowing water under two feet of clear ice where a bowfin glides.

"Will it die?" she asks.

"I think it can freeze like a frog."

Our shadows are ascended on the channel bed as we walk over the ice. Half-inch hoarfrost blades cover the fallen tree stuff strewn everywhere. They capture the light of the sun like exotic flames. Everything is engulfed in them, and Lily herself is like a rumored spirit with her white coat and gray eyes kindred elemental to it all, as if it was she who cast the winterfire over everything. We come to the cay of a pond and I go out until the ice cracks below me like lightning. Lily warns me back. A warning not to imply a dare, and I turn to her standing on the cay and we move on in no hurry at all, the both of us content on spending the days wandering the wilderness in the cold and snowless early winter of ninety-nine.

I told myself to remember. It has to sustain you forever, so take all you see and pair it with as many things as you can for easy recall. A vast number of such relations, and I do remember.

We arrive at her place well after noon. Lily opens the door and her mother is on the couch as always, wearing a chambray shirt and smoking a cigarette to the filter. She looks at us like we're strangers and says nothing, her temporary composer thin as tinfoil over the mouth of an active volcano. The moment I leave it'll go up. Sometimes even before I leave.

Lily's eyes flick to mine as if to say farewell without saying it, and then she darts to the stairs gripping the volute and vaulting the first two steps and scampering the rest. Her father hears and comes inside from the back catching only the wake of her in the white drapery of the landing door window. I stand there so he sees me, then I turn to leave.

"You need a ride?" he asks, before I can.

"No sir."

"Where the hell do you live?"

"Few miles south," I lie.

"What's your address?"

"I'm not supposed to give it out." The man runs his hand through the threads of his thin hair then he waves for me to follow him to the backyard. I do, under the tracking gaze of the mother mute on her grafted sofa. The smell of old food from somewhere. We enter a foyer and step through a large white door that's more ornate than the front one. The portico is in the midst of receiving a new coat of white paint. It occurs to me that over the years the back of the house became the front as the surrounding roads developed.

"You like to fight, huh?" he asks and points to his own left eye to indicate the bruise under mine.

"Oh," I say. "Just a game of touchdown toss."

"You don't have a problem with bullies do you?"

"No."

"Are you a bully?"

I shake my head, but I'm running the question through. "I don't pick on anyone smaller than me, if that's what you mean."

"Good, good," he smiles and takes a sip of Coricidin from an amber bottle. "Did you win?"

"The fight?"

"No, the lottery. Yes the fight, did you win?"

"Yeah."

He makes a show of looking doubtful with a squinting side-eye. "You don't strike me as someone to win fights."

"A lot of people think so too. That's why I win."

He laughs in waves. I can't help but smile just a little. "I like that. You get in trouble for fighting?"

"Sometimes, but mostly, no."

"What do your parents say about you getting in trouble for fighting?"

I shrug.

"What do they say?"

I wonder if Lily might be listening through the window, but I answer anyway: "They don't say much. Except for a couple times they don't really know, and I tell them I'm just clumsy."

"You tell them what you told me and they believe you?"

I nod.

The man smirks. "They know, kid. Or are you telling me they're cross-eyed stupid?"

I shrug again, becoming self-conscious of doing

it so much. "No, they're not stupid," I say. Thinking on it, they probably don't know what to do about it. I'd no intention of becoming distant with them, but it happened anyway. And this man and the women in there probably had no intention of hating each other either, but that also happened anyway.

"Listen," he says, hushed. "Lily brings around this other kid sometimes. Tall and stringy. You know him?"

A flash of adrenaline, there then gone. I shrug.

"Well, thing is, I don't want my daughter hanging around him. Lily's a small girl, she shouldn't pal around with boys who can't protect her. I've told him off but he won't take the hint, and now the only thing to be done about it will put me in for time, you understand? It's up to you. I'll mention also that Lily doesn't like him much either. She thinks he's a creep and is waiting for someone to do something about him, since she can't herself.

"Is that what she said?"

"No, but Dad's got a feeling for these things. She doesn't like the kid."

"She would have told me that."

"Not if she thinks you wouldn't do anything about it. Women are like that, they're silent about the things that hurt them. You ever notice that? And the way Lily acts around him. I don't know, ask her for me will you?" He swigs the last bit of medicine from the bottle and throws it into a toppled bin and makes some gesture as an end to our discussion, then he goes back inside.

A Beacon in the Light

The land slopes down and to the right, east I think, but there's no way to be sure. A stream runs near. Uluru in the rain. White veins down the arkose. Places I've never been and had never seen but through television screens. In this dreamscape there is light but no detail to anything. I keep the slope to my left for guidance but soon realize I'm tracing around a hill in circles and I sit onto the cold earth and reach behind my back for the tube and bite valve of my water pouch, but it's gone. Lost it in the river. I heard water somewhere a minute ago and I stand – too fast – the shadows change, the place and the time, seamless as if the wilderness led naturally to the brown acrylic floor tiles and plaster of the school hall.

He goes down the line of lockers testing the padlock's on each by yanking hard on them. One gives, and he opens it and peeks inside. A girl's locker. Inside are books and a bottle of sunscreen and he opens up the bottle and squirts some onto the books and then picks at the stickers and tears at the posters hung up inside. He grabs at something behind the books and pulls it out. It's a silver necklace. "Whatcha got there?" I say to him, satisfied with having returned his first words to me in kind. But something in the hall resonates with my voice, ringing with it, undermining it somehow. The kid wheels and pulls his hoodie from his head, eyes all narrow like he's squinting at the sun. I doubt there's ever a moment he doesn't look incensed. He's got a trail of pale freckles down his face like a Z taken at either end and pulled till the angles are obtuse. He tosses the necklace back into the locker and closes it then just stares at me for a while. I can tell usually tell if someone wants to fight or run by where their feet are pointing, and his are pointed right at me. He unshoulders his backpack and places it at his feet. His knuckles are pronounced and silvery with scars and his shins are marked with the pink remnants of scabs and more recent abrasions too. It seems there's nothing he won't do to prove how tough he is in spite of his deformity; that spine of his. It's clear I can't convince him that I'm more capable of violence than he is. There's an advantage in making your opponent believe you're crueler than they are, that you'll take it further than they will. No one wants to fight someone willing to do real harm. People will let you wail on them because they're afraid of what will happen if they fight back, and worse, what will happen if they win. But that isn't possible with him. "You're Avery, right?" he says.

I don't answer.

"Lily talks about you sometimes. Do you want to know what she says?"

"She doesn't say anything to you," I tell him. That ringing isn't coming from something in the hall. It's coming from something in my voice.

He smiles. "Of course she does. She told me you're going blind and that she's scared she'll have to lead you around everywhere. She wants me to scare you off, because she doesn't want to tell you to get lost herself. No girl wants to lead some boy around, don't you know that?"

A frightening rage shivers its way into my brain, my body. From the top pocket of my backpack I grab a dull pencil and drop the backpack at my feet holding the pencil in my hands like a shiv.

"How do you plan to use that?" he asks. His voice is quiet He doesn't want to alert the teachers in the classrooms whose voices carry out into the halls.

I look down at it. "I think I'll make you blind before me," I say. It's the truth. I'll hurt him for good.

"You know what I think?" he says. "I think you'd curl into a little ball and cry if real danger came to you. Most kids who fight are just playing. But I'm not." He's holding now a small knife he'd performed some sleight of hand to get there without my notice.

Down the hall from us a door swings open and there's the clip of kitten heels on the linoleum. "Avery, go to class now!"

I stay.

"Did you hear me? Class. Now! You too!" The teacher takes my arm and pulls me away. The kid is smiling at me.

I bring a hand to the gash in the back of my skull and find bulbs of congealed blood around the wound. On the slightest touch the pain lights up bright enough to see. I sit and remove the boot from my left foot, and the remaining wool sock too and ring-out the water then bundle it up and use the canvas belt buckle to tighten the sock around my head. What good will it do?

The bullet wound above my collarbone is in too awkward a place to dress easily. Dress it with what? I feel for blood but my clothes are still wet from the river. The pain has dulled. I rotate my shoulder and there's an impingement when I raise my arm above my head. Nothing to do about it.

I stand and go on. Go where? Through and through again the same dark frame with little change to it. The shadows of the land and the woods my mind conjures are somehow darker than the blackness behind them. Like passing your own limb in front of your eyes in a pitch black room and still perceiving it as an even deeper void. What makes that possible? Strange link between the brain and proprioceptors throughout the body?

Leaves shuffle off ahead of me, the both of us captive to the same wind, and we're taken into a ravine that opens to a flatland of coniferous trees. Hemlock, I think. We go into shallow water where the leaves drift down and are caught in the water and are drowned. Fallen trees all laying the same way. A flood came through here.

Spikelets have worked into my shoes and pant legs. There's a warmth on my right side. The sun has peeked over the horizon. How much of the night spent walking and how much of it sleeping? I go with the sun on my back now, and in some span of time, maybe an hour, my outstretched hand crumples against the wood paneling of a decaying structure.

Frank

We take vantage on a jut of granite over the river. I glass the land below with the binoculars where the river winds off into the shadowed woods to Beartrap Lake, which appears as a dim cut of sky under the horizon. From there begin new rivers which go to yet more lakes, on and on east to Lake Superior.

I lower the binoculars and steady my gaze, holding still so that anything that moves is revealed against everything that's still. But all that moves is the river. This could be where we lose him.

"What do you think?" asks Tanner.

I fold the binoculars up and stuff them in the inside pocket of my fall calico ghillie. "I think if you could swim I'd have tossed you in after him."

We begin down to the water, Tanner trailing.

"I'm telling you I got him," he says. "You saw the way he fell? Like a bag of bricks." He claps his hands to simulate the sound. "No way he gets throat-shot then survives flood rapids."

"Unless he's not throat-shot."

"I saw the man's neck blasted out when he fell. It's adrenaline. Like deer short of a shot to the brain. They'll run with a gaping hole in their heart for half a mile before going down. I bet he's dead downriver."

"Then we'll find him dead downriver. But he isn't dead. A man hit bad will crumple around the wound and go down like you said, but he didn't go down like that. He was startled off balance is all."

"I think he went down exactly like that."

"You're not interested in making sure?"

"We'll get ourselves caught making sure, is what

I think."

"Now you want to be cautious? What happened to the man dashing headlong into the shadows and thorn-brush by himself?" I ask. Nothing. Only slow and clumsy footsteps in answer, like a dejected child marching off to the bedroom he's been grounded to. "This mess is your own damn fault. You couldn't wait for us and lost your rifle to the man. You took the shot before I did when I told you clear, only to shoot after.

"Well, I got my rifle back. And I'll say it again, I got him. You'll see," he says unconvincingly.

"The man gave it back. What I think is you assume you'll strike some deal with the police when they catch up to you."

"What the hell kind of deal are you talking about?"

I turn to take a long look at him. His face is pleasingly symmetrical, like it's reflected down the middle by a mirror. All features of it are divisible by one or one-half of another, and his brows are flat across the ridge of his forehead in an expression as neutral as your first take of his disposition. How different his life would be had he any intelligence at all, or any temperament. "You're young. You can play for sympathy and say we coerced you. Police will promise a better sentence and you'll take it, and take much more locked away with us regardless."

He spits. "No I wouldn't." From his argyle shirt pocket he takes a fresh plug of tobacco and packs his cheek. I shake my head at him and go on. He says nothing for a time but then he says, "He's pretty dumb too you know. Just handin' us the gun when it was all what stopped us from running up on him."

"Maybe he can't shoot for shit like you," I say. "So he used it the only way he could. And it worked, didn't it?" He doesn't respond. "Did it work or not?"

"It worked," he mumbles. "But it only bought him time to-"

"Quiet," I whisper.

Movement in the woods on the other side of the river. I drop to a knee and Tanner does the same. Passing through the trees is a figure, combining with the shadows of its surroundings and is lost. I scope in, scanning the duff, and I spot the pale make of a face to the ground and behind the scope of its own rifle, the barrel sweeping to me. Before he can sight me I let out a low whistle. The man freezes then returns with a whistle of his own. We emerge from cover and come to opposite sides of the river.

"I almost popped you," gloats Tanner.

"Anything?" I ask in a voice just loud enough to travel the waters.

"Nothing. Gave ECPD a goose chase and came this way," says Glen.

"Heli passed over two hours ago. Tricks won't work for much longer," I say.

"Don't you think he's drowned?" asks Glen.

"He's not drowned," I say. "Might have rode the rapids to calmer water then swam ashore. He'd have taken the first opportunity, so I'm thinking in a couple miles we'll find his prints off the bank somewhere."

Glen nods and begins east, parallel with us for a

distance then he draws back into the woods when the cut of the river becomes too steep. Tanner and I track along the very edge of it, where man-sized chunks of clay collapse inches from our feet into the black water when we pass. The river opens and the water slows. Its banks becoming undefined and intermingled within swards of highgrass. We explore the edges of these pools for tracks but there are none. Farther on down there's a fishing boat foundered near the rooted stem of an ash tree. In it is a tackle box, the contents spinning sedately in a captured current. An easterly wind comes with the rising sun and with it the sour reek of fish and droppings from thousands of waterfowl. We travel beyond the flooded lands where the river narrows again, its currents braiding together into short sprints of rapids. Unwinding, narrowing again. "I thought you said he'd have taken the first opportunity?" says Tanner. "He probably followed a splay to conceal his tracks back there."

"Might have."

The river opens again, running now at a pace hardly faster than a jog. I catch the tracks in the emerging light of the sunrise, distinguishable as the clashing contrails of high-flying passenger jets against the sky. Tanner thinks he saw them first and points them out silently with the rifle then he takes the lead.

"Go into the water," I say. "He came this way. We don't want to confuse his tracks with our own."

Tanner obeys and cuts out of the berm and goes to the prints, treading the water. "He dragged himself out," says Tanner. We follow to the treeline and I whistle for Glen and he comes from the trees and I point to the tracks. He nods. Tanner kneels on the heels of his feet and points to a body print in the mud and says "See? He's hurt."

"Of course he's hurt. So keep your voice down. He could be close."

"Naw, he's not armed, else he'd have used it on me."

The kid is naive. "Men are always armed," I tell him. "With their limbs and with their teeth and what they get close enough to take from you. When you forgot that your rifle became *his* rifle." I glance back at him but he's looking away, embarrassed.

We follow onto a maze of tracks. The man they belong to is either delirious or this is some attempt to confuse us, and as if to take it from my mind, Tanner says, "No way he knew he'd have time to do all this. I think he's lost."

The tracks trend more and more to the west as he regained his senses. It was the sun, I realize. He was confused from exhaustion and injury, but the sun rose and gave him direction again.

"He's not hiding, he's hightailing it back to Flint Road," I say. "We're an hour behind him. Thirty minutes if we hurry."

Tanner grins. "I can keep up."

We set off at a jog.

Sean

The stack of case records grows in the corner. By now it's clear my prior knowledge of the Weakling Killings represents the extent of what knowledge there is. With nothing left for me to do here I leave the room in disarray and walk in the silence and near-dark of the understory. The high windows on the east wall glow with a faint gray light but pass little of it into the dark. At the center of the floor however is a lone fluorescent, and in the fringes of its light glint the metallics of chairs and desks and office supplies stacked like forts put up by children against the threat of the darkness down here.

I go to the concourse and out the front doors into the morning air and take it in. But I've only taken my frustrations to the parking lot; to the curbs clinging onto crumbling yellow facades; the sodium-yellow light of the street lamps captured in a thin fog and the changing traffic signals conducting no one through the empty avenues in the early quiet when nocturnal things have gone to their burrows and day things have yet to rise; after atmospheric imbalances have resolved and before the sun can disturb them again.

Aaron had been a suspect for as long as it took the coroner to determine time of death and for his partner to alibi him. It happens that on September ninth he was at the station conducting his very own interview for a case involving a drunken boat accident. He was there all day, going for lunch to strategize with his partner who substantiated. Irrefutable, unless I'm to suspect half the department. Aaron could not have been there when they were killed. And what new information have I found that would spark investigation into the man? William dead, there's nothing but a disagreement between colleagues. The eventual discovery of William's body will at most be a lesson. Some may remark that we should have done better. Aaron might lose his position as Chief of Ely City Police and William's demise will be added to our list of unsolved murders. Time will do its work on what artifacts remain and then there will be nothing but records to read and to be confounded by.

If it's desperation that informs my actions here on, let it be so, and with some unidentified resolve I return inside and to Gibbs' desk and find him hovering over a steaming cup of black coffee. He's a regular house mouse like Aaron and I but for reasons other than professionalism. "Did you sleep?" I ask him.

He looks up at me beseechingly. "Some. Good Christ, why?"

"I need you with me."

"Where to? Aren't you reassigned?"

"It's nothing to do with the search effort."

"At least tell me where we're going."

"The McLloyd home."

"You're hoping to find William there, aren't you?"

"Maybe. Will you back me up or not?"

The road has been untraveled for years. Deadwood litters the way. In the driver's seat, Gibbs lights himself a cigarette and holds the carton out to me and I wave it away. "Don't have but the one vice do you?" he says, then pockets the cigarettes.

"What's the one vice?"

"Pissing off Aaron." He rolls his window down and the smoke from his cigarette ropes out of it. Logs here and there on the road. They break to mulch under the tires, but then we come to a downed shagbark bridging the waysides far too big to simply drive over. Gibbs swings us to the side of the road and we idle there for a time. "You know this is a twenty-man job right?" he says.

"Only us to spare."

"There's a manhunt on. Armed and dangerous, the whole deal."

"We're armed too."

"And I've got your back and all, but why not wait for things to cool down?"

"For what to cool down? The danger or the bodies?"

He looks at me and flicks his cigarette butt out the window and fishes the carton from his front pocket and lips another from it, lights the end in one action as natural to him as breathing. "So this *is* about William."

"The manhunt is related. Parallel. But no, it's not about William."

"What's it about?" He grabs the carbine from its mounted holster on the back of my seat then he climbs out from the truck. I step out and go to the bed and pluck the chainsaw from under the tarpaulin.

"It's about Aaron."

"Chief?"

"That's the one." We go to the fallen shagbark and he stands close with his carbine held high ready.

"Hold the light," I tell him, but his eyes are passing over the pale obscurities around us. "Haven't you noticed the way he's been going about all this, in comparison to other missing persons cases, I mean?"

Gibbs shrugs and says with half his mouth given to the cigarette, "I'd be doing things differently, yeah."

"What would you be doing differently?"

He chews the side of his cheek. "Well, I'd have hired every news and private helicopter in the area to go looking. I'd have assumed a twenty mile search radius from the get."

I nod. "Right. But Aaron's treated William as dead and the killers as long gone since the beginning."

"Blind man running from multiple people who want him that way. I can understand the assumption," says Gibbs.

"So can I. That's why it's the perfect pretext to let it happen."

"Anything can be twisted that way," says Gibbs. "Why would he want that?"

"William knows something about the McLloyd murders Aaron would rather he die with."

Gibbs shakes his head. "Aaron is just doing a poorer job than you'd like."

"Maybe."

"Probably."

"Have it your way."

"What do you hope to find after twenty-four years?"

"Don't know. Hold the light." He does and I yank the pullstart and the engine barks and the chain thrashes on the bar. I press the blade through the stem of the downed tree, and when it's done we drag the two halves to the sides just enough to pass through them.

"Hate making noise when nothing else is," whispers Gibbs.

We go to the truck and I put the chainsaw under the tarp again and climb in and move on meticulously down the road. "On principle?"

"I guess so. If it's quiet so am I."

"Not a bad habit as yours go."

We take an enjoined dirt road a couple miles north then Gibbs swings us left onto a driveway hardly distinguishable under the leaves and mud. We idle there. Gibbs checks his carbine again and I, my SIG Sauer. The old home is sealed shut with particle board. Faded signs nailed on all ground-floor entries warning against trespass. There are two hooded windows on the upper floors like eyes. The porch hip is held up by thin columns, and it looks like someone took an ax and tried to topple them. On the porch sits a dirt-caked camera case. Probably belongs to some social media clairvoyant who came here to make contact with one of the family members. Even the public suspects the McLloyd family home to be the true scene of their murders. Most of the time they fancy to have spoken with the daughter. Her voice suggested in the random static of EVP devices, giving vague descriptions of the one who killed her and no more.

I climb out and so does Gibbs and we wrap swiftly around the house and meet at the rear. Gibbs shakes his head and I go back to the truck for bolt cutters. There's a wooden shack leaning from true on the old driveway. A padlock on the hasp, rust stains all down the door. I cut the lock off and push the door open, the bottom of it digging into the damp earth. Inside, arachnids everywhere. Clumps of Harvestmen untangling themselves from fur-like congregations and skittering away from the light of the emerging day. I step inside among them, shining my own light at the shadows. Nothing but an emptied workbench, well-worn with decades' worth of chattermarks and layers of paint. The smell of lacquer off the walls. My feet are covered in the Harvestmen.

"Find what you're looking for?" calls Gibbs.

"I don't know what I'm looking for." We go to the front entrance, Gibbs with his head like a wind vane in a thunderstorm. "They'd be stupid to fire on us," I tell him.

"Criminals aren't known for their intelligence."

I shoulder through what remains of the particle board in place of the door. Inside the air has sat still as the interior of quartz crystal. And now the open way disturbs that brittle stillness, and all the cobwebs spanning the spaces between things bend to me as one, and break. An even layer of dust coats everything but where the wind scratches through unsealed gaps in the boarded windows and the doors, and there, little braids of dust propagate a short distance like clips of tawny hair. We step inside like abridging some malediction. The floorboards groan and something scratches behind the walls. Our lights dance between the shadows, guns at the ready. Ready for what?

There's an RCA television against the west wall. The kind made to look like furniture. Antique even in the nineties. Opposite this is a yellowed floral-patterned sofa, sunken in the middle from long use as a bed. The dining table is a metal square with worn argyle fabric stitched over the top. Four wooden chairs arranged neatly on all sides. In the kitchen stands a red vintage refrigerator. Plates and bowls made in Tennessee stacked in the cabinets on either side of it. Inherited things, if I'd guess.

A staircase ascends the north wall. The wooden steps croak and splinter a little as I climb to the mezzanine. An empty console table stands below a painting of a corsair with torn sails thrashing in the waves against its shoring. Above the painting is an awning window tapped over with worn masking. The upper landing is blocked with particle board. I tell Gibbs to get an ax from the truck and he brings it up and I hack it all down. From the sealed upper story comes a breath of stale air like from a tomb. There are two bedrooms and a bath. In the master is a neatly done queen flanked by twin dressers. An armoire with clothing inside: jean jacket and a woman's coat from American Airlines. The second bedroom has a single twin bed and an opened and empty foot locker with a matching white dresser. An enjoined bath with a medicine cabinet missing its mirror. Not shattered, simply gone.

In the ceiling of the landing hall there's a hatch to the attic. The pulldown string is tucked inside. I drag the footlocker from the bedroom under it and step up and fish my fingers into the space between the hatch and ceiling panels and find the string and pull it and the hatch swings down with tufts of clotted dust curling to the floor. I fold out the ladder and climb up. Daylight picks into the darkness from a dormer window half covered with green tarp. I want to see it as it has sat here so I turn my light off and climb up and stand very still to avoid disturbing the fragile galaxies of dust twisting through the rays and those of them unseen in the dark. This place was her own. Here and there are foraged things: Tinware; an empty wooden box lined with red baize and a recess for a ceremonial pen; a pile of water-smoothed wooden sculptures, nature made; sticks that look like deer antlers, like dolls, like people, or that just look interesting; books of no common kind, fiction and encyclopedia intermingled. There's a small table and chair under the dormer window, the mirror for the medicine cabinet hung above it. Near these is a pillowtop mattress on the floor, over which a white sheet is propped on a clothes line strung up between the cornering walls as a little fort. A fort against what?

Hold your breath and move only the eyes. Make no sound. Like a particle that behaves differently unobserved, so do the shadows here. If there's anywhere to moor devastation it's in a place like this. Sit awhile. Years' worth of it arriving all of a sudden. This was no ordinary refuge of the kind all children devise out of cardboard boxes or sheets and coach pillows in the living room. She lived here, in this attic. Scratchings on the walls. Drawings etched into the wood. Am I reading too much into what I see here? Maybe. But I know that

I'd have hid away in this place too, had I an attic to do so. Instead I had an unused garage. No air vents to carry the moans into there. It did well enough.

I think she'd sit there under the window, and on her days off from school the sun would beam through the window and touch down onto the desk just before noon, where she'd be sitting, like something growing advantageously within the track of daylight into a dark and hidden place.

She didn't sleep in the room below. Instead, she'd tuck the string for the hatch up into the attic as I found it, safe up here. But why have I imagined the family in conflict with itself? They all died the same way: They died together, at the hands of another.

I stand and thumb through the books and sift through the piles of things, but there's nothing revelational contained in them. I lift the mattress where only dust and beetles hide underneath. What am I looking for?

"You okay up there?" shouts Gibbs through the floor.

"Yeah."

"Have you found anything?"

"Have I found anything?"

"Yeah."

There's a leak from the roof running in a black and rotten vein to the floor, and probably down the inner walls to the foundation. The raw wooden desk is paled under the dust, and a composition booklet too. I pick it up. Stuffed regularly between the pages are homework assignments dated in pencil to the very week of her death. Much of the writings are incomprehensible, but from what I can read it's clear this was no diary of hers that might give insights. In the drawer of the table are sketches and some Polaroids scattered randomly inside. I gather up the photos and sift through each carefully like they might dissolve in my hands. Most are faded except for those of them that were face down or protected under another photo or page. Mostly they are pictures of rare bugs and a couple are of Lily herself putting in effort to look pretty. These too were taken by William, but otherwise they give me nothing except confirmation that they were close. I place them back into the drawer and close it.

I tear the green tarp from the window, and the sun now projects a distorted shape of it onto the slanted sidewall. Through the window, Gibbs has gone back to the truck and is radioing something in, but I've turned my own radio off and can't hear what. The flights of dust particles in the air have slowed and nearly solidified again in the time I've stood here. If there's a word for the feeling that a thing will not be seen by human eyes for a long time I don't know it. It's a feeling of its very own.

I return to the hatch and climb down and then down the stairs to the ground floor. Gibbs is waiting in the living room, arms crossed and his rifle held between them against his chest. "Well?" he says.

"Well what?"

He squints at me. "Are you alright?"

I go past him to the front door. The sun is coming through it now and through the small cracks in the window boards. Needles of light into the darkness. Onto the table. The TV. The sofa. Recognition. From where? Too much in the mind.

"What is it?" asks Gibbs.

Age-yellowed fabric and a pink floral pattern. And adjacent to the couch are scars on the wooden floor panels where the matching love seat must have sat for years. A similar love seat is pictured in one of the photos I'd left at HQ. A photo of an unknown home over the water... "We need to get back. Fast."

"Christ, what's the rush now?"

I move past Gibbs and out the door. He follows. "I can't say," I tell him.

"Why not?"

"If I say it, it won't be true."

"You aren't superstitious."

"No, but I'm in a hurry."

William

The vague stench of black tar heroin comes off the plaster walls. There is no door and I step up into the structure and swing my feet out an inch from the floor to make way. Cans and glass bottles everywhere, clattering hollowly into piles of more detritus. "Anyone here?" I say. There is no return but my own voice off the rotten walls. Something moves in the attic. A raccoon or squirrel sojourned up there. To be sure I take a can from the floor and underhand it into the roof. Plaster comes down and the animal scampers through some escape and leaps into the leaves outside and is gone. I trace the left wall to a brick mantle and kneel and reach to touch the cold remains of embers on the andiron. I pat the floor around the fireplace and find dry wood under a tarp and grab three logs and toss them on the hearth then search under the tarp for kindling and find bundled newspaper and stuff it between the logs. I search the mantle for something to light it up. On it are broken beer bottles and shot-through cans and soggy card stock cartons. Each of these I take and rattle their contents inside. Most of them contain stagnant water. Some hold caps or nails or bullet shells. One contains a wad of plastic grocery bags held with a rubber band. I undo it and a bundle of matchsticks spills over my hands and scatters onto the ground. I kneel and drag my cold fingertips over the floor, feeling little but what pierces the skin like a splinter or shard of glass. I find one of the matches and relocate the carton and strike a flame and swing it carefully to the bundled newspaper in the fireplace.

Warmth blooms around my hands, my arms and face, and the flames take hold onto the wood. The heat popping the pockets of moisture trapped in the grain. Smoke fills the room. I forgot to open the flue so I reach into the firebox and pull the lever for the smoke to escape high above the trees for everyone to see for miles. I stay for some time for warmth, but I can't stay for long. They will come soon, everyone, the police and the hunters together. But I won't be here, since it will probably be the hunters who come first. The meeting arranged, I stand and leave into the woods.

<u>Frank</u>

Smoke rises above the horizon a quarter mile to the east. I motion to it for the others and Glen says, "What are the chances he's that stupid?"

"He's betting police are closer than we are," I say.

"He bet wrong," says Tanner. But far in the distance are helicopter blades chopping sharply at the air.

"Now or never," says Glen and the man of forty years checks his weapon over and looks at me and the two of us bound into a run, gliding through the trees and looking for the shape of a man limping from the old home now coming into view. A clearing surrounds the place. We keep to the trees round to the other side but there's no sign the man is still here. No obvious prints heading away from the place either. I step into the building with my weapon raised but there's no one. Just muddy tracks on the floorboards and a fire blazing in the hearth, spitting cinders onto the floor and belching smoke into the room. He's just a few minutes in any direction, but the helicopter is minutes from us too.

Glen and Tanner rush in through the front entrance, their excitement gone when they see it's only me in here. Tanner wags his head and looks at the fire and at the muddy prints on the floor, and he makes some reckoning of the chopper outside. "They'll catch us before we catch him. I think we should high-tail out of here. We'll bush it for a long time. Maybe we'll go to the city."

Us. We.

"Even if they have drawings of our faces, people don't think that long about such things in the city like they do here."

Our faces. "Just let me think," I tell him, and I kneel to the worn wood of the abandoned cabin. The roof is still partially intact. Fire would spread easily up there.

"C'mon, are we just gonna sit here?" Tanner asks. The blades of that helicopter are close, a couple miles. It angles in on a direct path to us now. They'll have eyes-on in a minute or so. "What are we doing guys?" he asks on the edge of a scream. Hidden in the motion of standing and re-slinging my rifle, I shoot him in the chest. Quick and surreptitious. Hardly saw it coming myself, so how could he? Tanner lets out a sigh of defeat like he's lost a game of cards, and he falls. No blood. Glen watches him struggling on the ground, watches him attempt to stand and perhaps to look at us watching him. His consciousness wanes and his body is taken by impulse now, the brain firing every neuron in all directions and then he's gone.

"I'll give you that he looks like the guy," says Glen. "It's prudent to ask though: would it have been me if I looked like him?"

"You'd have seen it coming," I say. He makes no move to shoulder his rifle and just holds it in one hand to the ground. He doesn't really need to point it at me. A flick of the wrist and he is, and my own rifle at him as quickly. "We're here because of him. No, I wouldn't have done it to you," I tell him. I go to the fireplace and take a burning stick from it and pass the flame to anything that will take it. The fire leaps into the rafters, blackening the walls, the paper curling and flaking to ashes and the heat becomes too much to stand in an instant.

Sean

We're heading back on Pineshire Way when I see the smoke as a thin gray spire over the trees to the north. The smoke turns black and whips up with an immense heat into the morning air. The outer plumes cool and stall out and the hot center charges on. Avian One cracks over the radio to report it and I snatch the mic from the dash and tell them we're seventy-six. Gibbs guns it, the tires raking out new fringes in the seldom traveled road. We're back on Highway One in five minutes, howling northbound with the wind whistling through the imperfect seals in the doors. In three miles we turn off onto another road, the serpentine of it seen in the tops of the trees more so than on the ground. We carve over deadwood and push through a swivel gate and soon, glimpses of bright flame can be seen through the trees. Avian One is making halos around the column of smoke. "Look for anyone fleeing the area," I say into the radio. The pilot affirms.

We stop some fifty yards from the burning structure and climb out and do a sweep of the area, but there's no one. The blades of the helicopter thwack the cold air like a drum. Another approaches, an S-Seventy that swings out above us and douses the fire with hundreds of gallons of lake water from a hanging bucket. The flames sputter and white steam erupts from the structure, but the orange glow of fire remains shimmering through the interstices. The chopper touches down in a clearing and offloads its helitack crew equipped with chainsaws and each an ax in hand. They encircle the structure and go to work sawing down dead trees susceptible to the flames then dragging them away. After a while the S-Seventy returns with another bucket-full of water, pulling sharply upward with the monsoon bucket swinging out ahead. The payload is released and it descends in a shimmering white spear that shatters the rooftop, but the fire remains. It takes four buckets to extinguish it. The firemen are standing by now, peering into the smoke-dried canopies above with diligence on their faces. Their Captain approaches Gibbs and I, shouting commands into his radio, then he says to us, "You guys smell that?"

"Smells like a barbecue, Captain, " I say. The grim recognition is shared silently between the three of us. "So what's the rush?"

The man jerks his head, his leatherhead lagging behind the gesture. "There's still fire somewhere. We'll have to wait for a truck."

"How long?"

"Twenty minutes," he says, then goes back to his men.

Avian One turns sharp to the east and vanishes behind the peaks of coniferous trees and there's silence enough to listen to the cracking flames somewhere under the structure. A mile off emergency lights flap over the trees along the highway and down the old road. No sirens. The fire truck turns down the macadam road, the weight of it rocking over debris. It stops in the clearing the helicopter landed in before. A fireman mounts the stang monitor and arcs water onto the ashen frame. Another unfurls lengths of hose in parallel bands on the ground while the nozzle team beams water through what's left of the windows. Five of them, equipped with oxygen canisters harnessed to their backs, enter the building seeking remnants of fire and victims. The captain comes to us again and says, "Got a body. Male."

Gibbs calls it in.

I have to see it for myself, so I go at once to the entrance of the blackened and dripping ruins and peer inside. It's lying by the fireplace, hardly distinguishable from the crozzled debris fallen around it. The skin is cooked taught around the bone. It's face is down among the billets, arms tucked under the torso and permanently heat-tempered there. His feet are bare and his toes are all curled inward like a beef patty overcooked on one side.

Gibbs comes up behind me. "Lock the area down," I tell him. "Nothing in or out. All of it under ice and everything documented. I want this place to be found as it is a hundred years from now, understand?" Gibbs nods, and he goes first to the group of firemen with their gear strewn about at their feet and he asks them if there's still fire. They stand and gather their equipment and pack it in the firetruck. Gibbs and I coordinate preservation efforts, flagging what we can before more backup arrives. When the Medical Examiner comes he and I pull on gloves and roll the body; reduced blood pulling at the clothes like syrup. There's a gunshot wound to his chest. His face is scorched and totally unrecognizable. Death sheds the layers from the soul as a rule, but death by fire most of all, bringing it screaming against the blackened skin like a failed exorcism.

The examiner kneels to the body, smirking to himself, aware, I think, of some contrivancy as to the need of his presence here. "Here I thought he still had a chance," he says, and crumples his cap around his eyes against the sun. I take a silver pen from the examiner's shirt pocket and use it to prod the pockets of the dead man and find nothing in them. "Anyway, looks pretty dead to me so he's yours," he says, and takes his pen from me then leaves.

The body is packed and air-lifted to the mortuary. With nothing more to do, Gibbs and I leave in the Rover. Word spreads fast over radio. The rescue teams presently combing over miles of woodland report no sign of William, chiming in one after the other on hearing of the body as some tacit corroboration between each of them that it's all over. Everybody is signing off. Finished chasing ghosts.

We arrive back at the station and I'm like a ball bearing in a balancing maze. Things must be done faster than they can be. A deep bone DNA analysis cross-referenced with samples taken from William's hair and charges drawn up against Aaron for obstruction, but DNA results won't come back for twenty-four hours and I have nothing on Aaron but a question he can shrug away, and then I'm done like everyone else is. I hardly remember the photo of the boathouse on my desk, and when I do, and go into my office to get it I find that it's gone. All the photos are. Aaron must have them, but for now I sit awhile with the feeling of being suspended between two fast-moving parts. Frozen with thinking. Thinking of thinking. I want to burst into Aaron's office and snatch the damn photos from his hands and demand answers but that isn't the play. He's sitting in there now. His movements, tics, translated into the squeaky piston of his desk chair. How do I approach this?

He knows the tricks. He knows never to fill a silence with unsolicited details. To hold himself openly and to avoid protective posturing. He knows I'll lie to him. Mostly he knows these are games. None of it means a thing as long as his story is brief and does not contradict with the evidence. That there is no benefit in confessing to any crime no matter what I might say. Anyone involved in police work has thought to themselves, *If ever I'm facing the door of an interrogation room, I'll know what to do.* We come to learn that a concise or silent subject is far more impenetrable than any with a good lie. But I'm getting ahead of myself. There is no interrogation. Now get the photos.

I stand and enter his office through the side door. He's ruminating over an old map of Ely and a paper cup of coffee. The photos are nowhere in sight. He doesn't even look up at me. "None of it is on the maps anymore," he says. "You know that? The Camp. Pineshire or Flint Road. North Valley."

The door closes hard behind me and he looks up and grabs at his coffee. "Everyone left," I say.

He sets down the coffee without drinking any and folds his arms. "Have you come to tell me what I should have done?"

I sit. "No need. In your desk is a Polaroid photo William took of a boathouse with furniture that matches what's in your brother's home. I think it's where he's going now."

He straightens minutely like ice has been touched to his back, then quickly settles again and is still. But the effort to keep from reacting is one itself. "Didn't I reassign you?" he says. Accompanying this is a little smile. He opens the center drawer of his desk and pulls out the stack of photos and sifts through them. When he finds the one he waves it at me then studies it for a time. "What is it you're talking about?"

"Through the window. The loveseat is the same make as the sofa in Daniel's home."

"Not through the window, through an opened door," he says. "You have any idea where this is?"

"I was hoping you might."

He shakes his head and puts the photo down. I take it and study it for myself. It's grainy and blurred somewhat, taken just after sundown. There's an orange contrail arcing over the boathouse. The structure stands on stilts half over the water and the smeared capture of the lake has the appearance of a thing added to the picture with pencil. Through the open front door is the love seat with the pink floral pattern. There's no one in the picture. "I went to his home," I say. "Everything in it's antique. Did he inherit the place?"

"His wife did. From her mother." Aaron's phone rings in his pocket and he slides it out and checks the screen and silences it then puts it on the desk.

"Daniel must have wanted a place of his own."

"I think so, but what I knew of his life was only spoken by him in defense of it. He always used to say I'd be twice as screwed had I gone through half what he had," says Aaron. "He said that we're gravely harmed being brought to life, some more than others, but all of us." I get the sense the last was not spoken by Daniel, but is something Aaron has come to believe about his brother's psychology through much rumination. Aaron stands and goes to the pot of coffee on a stainless file cabinet and drains the last of it into his cup, then he sits down again, all of it done with no amount of haste.

"How is it he was harmed?" I ask him.

Aaron looks at me with amused skepticism and he takes a drink, the coffee spilling out over his chin, over his hand. "It doesn't matter now. The man is dead."

"Of course it matters."

"Does it? William is dead, too. He's lying in the morgue awaiting autopsy."

"Awaiting identification. Until then I'll assume he's alive if it suits you. But even if it's him down there, I think these recent murders have something to do with what happened back then."

Aaron smiles. "I don't think so."

"Explain."

"It isn't possible."

"Why's that?"

His fingers articulate slightly in the air and then he moves his hand to the coffee again, but evidently changes his mind and brings it back to his chest. Parasympathetic ticks that are tells of actions that do not wholly materialize, things that do not break over the threshold from an act thought of to an act performed. Maybe I've shut him down? I think he wants to tell me something, and all I have to do is prove to him it matters to. He thinks William is dead. He thinks he'll incriminate himself if he goes on. Incriminate himself in what? I'm no longer sure. I take up the photo of the boathouse and flip it around to him. "All you have to do is remember. Take another look. Make a guess if you don't know, and we'll take it from there," I tell him. It's an out. If he knows where it is, by framing his admission as a 'guess' he's not admitting to anything at all. He knows that though, and takes the photo from my hand and stares at the picture for a very long while; the passing time becoming increasingly known to us both, antagonistically so, and at last he places the photo down and meets my eyes with the look of a man unpersuaded.

William

At my feet is the corrugation of a field tilled for crops, crowded now with wild ferns and weeds. I travel perpendicular to the plow lines. Beyond the field I find no house or barn and turn back onto the field and go with the lines and into the ruins of the farmhouse. The walls encroached around me from nowhere, and the notion I'd entered it developed over the course of ten or so paces without running into the stem of a tree. Toppled shiplap rattles where I step. There is no way to go quietly through here, and we have tried to come and leave without notice, but every door and every window, and even the shingles of the porch roof give us away each time.

Wrong time. Wrong place.

It's raining. There's no cover from it in the farmhouse and the large drops come through the crumbling roof to make instruments of everything: ringing lightly on a cast iron pot and tapping on the wooden rafters and nicking the masonry of a stone oven. It's very cold. It could be night again.

There's a screen door near the oven punched through at the bottom by animals. I crawl through the opening onto a porch where plants hang from fine chains. A cascade of brittle vines to the ground. The plants have been dead a long time sequestered in the hanging clay pots. I step from the patio onto fallen leaves, and not far from the farmhouse I come to a dirt road and follow it to an unfinished cul de sac. The ground has been leveled and there are stacks of two-by-fours and turning squares strewn everywhere.

I recall then that Daniel had been fixing up the old boathouse for a while and much of the deck was new wood. He asked if I'd like to help him and I agreed, but what I really wanted was for a bad storm to come through. A once in a century microburst to come rolling through to carve the place from the land for good. It was too close to the Promontory.

In a field I stumble over the lumber of a fallen silo. How long have I been walking? In what direction? Half of the reservoir is buried in the clay. The top is gone and someone used it as a shelter recently. The faint smell of char inside. I can't stay.

An owl calls high in a network of branches, all of them loping to the ground as if to support their own weight in a rootless migration elsewhere. I'd like to sleep under them but sleep is impossible sopping wet and thirty minutes at most ahead of those hunters. I go on. A shadow walks past me, rushes past, bending the branches into itself like a field of gravitation. It curls its fingers as if to gather the stands of wire that are strung to my body.

The rain stops. Her hair is flat and dark against her neck and she looks so much like her mother that way, and knows it. She gathers her hair over her shoulder and drains it of water, then her hands perform some legerdemain to make herself unlike her mother in seconds. She looks at me as if aware I made the relation. She has no one whose likeness to model her own after. Only her mother's to model against, and that's suitable enough. The fall leaves are bright with the rain and the branches are dark against them. She walks as I showed her, "Quiet like cats' paws on the carpet," I said, and we see foxes and an owl in an oak tree.

My mind leaps again, from one time to the next. Days, weeks, or months in one bound. I have no say in it now that I am lost.

I come into view of her place. The windows gazing back as always. But I know the people inside are never looking out from the windows. All their attention goes in.

Lily wasn't at school today. I've come from Hakon's place some miles away to find out why. There are dried tracks of mud going in and out of the open front door. I rap lightly on it and the mother snaps her head to me and stares, her mouth a contorted oval. "Tell him to leave," she croaks. The misshapen woman takes a long drag from her cigarette and turns away from me. Daniel comes down, his lips puckered like he's just woken up.

"She isn't here," he says.

"Where is she?"

"The hospital." He goes to the back and waves me to follow. I do, through the living room with the woman watching me like it's a trespass. Daniel leans against the porch railing. "You take care of that kid? What was his name?" he asks.

"Why is Lily in the hospital?"

"She's not hurt bad or anything. A sprained elbow. I'll be going soon to pick her up if you want to come." The man is out of it again on the medicine. I don't want to go anywhere with him but I don't want Lily to be alone with him either, so I nod. "Anyway, says she fell or something, but I think it was that kid. So what'd you do?"

"I talked to him."

"You mean you gave him a chance to lie to you. What did he say?" he asks.

I realize now that when I confronted the kid I'd forgotten why. We traded threats and nothing more. I shrug.

"What does that mean?"

"I don't think he's doing anything bad to her," I say.

"Have you asked her about it?"

"No, but he doesn't seem like he'd do that."

"Then you got a better sense of character than I do." He laughs.

"Have you asked her?" I say. He shoots a look at me with intensity, like he's sizing me up and wondering if he could get away with striking me across the mouth.

"Of course I have. In case you haven't noticed, things aren't okay here. Lily hardly talks to us anymore. I was hoping she might talk to you but I guess you're not him."

"Not who?"

"Not the guy she talks to. Every girl's gotta have one, but you're not it," says Daniel.

"It's probably another girl who she talks to about those things," I say.

Daniel shakes his head. "Lily's never gotten along with girls. Her mother scared her away from them. She thinks all of them eventually become like her mom. But it's not Emily. She says things to Lily sometimes but never touches her. The woman gets all of her anger out on me." Daniel lifts his brown hair away from his ear to show a cut on the side of his head spotted with black flakes of dried blood. "She used an ashtray," he says. "Anyway, if I found out it's her I'd kill her on the spot. You ever get like that?"

"Like what?"

"Like you would burn the world down for someone?"

I shrug. Thunder far away. Through the trees the sky is gray and there is no feature to it, just an average of its colors, like a camera in a dark house aimed at a bright window. "We should go," says Daniel and he takes a set of keys from his pocket and we walk around the house to the driveway where a pickup sits on partly deflating tires. Dead leaves are piled under the windshield where it meets the hood. Daniel brushes them off. Next to the truck there's an open shed with spare car parts rusted and ignored for years. A wood ax and a weed whacker too. Daniel pads drunkenly to the shed and closes it shut.

We fly up the thin road into Ely at fifty an hour. Daniel lets me keep the window down and he rolls his down with the rain coming in to soak the edges of our seats. He asks about school and about my friends and my parents. I answer, aloof. He tells me about his time in Asia, how he had been sent to fight because he wasn't in college like his brother. He says he'd been convinced not to go to school by his teachers who thought he was a bad student. They told him to get a job outside since he was so claustrophobic. Then he asks if I'll go to college. I tell him that my parents have planned that far but not me. He laughs.

We arrive at the hospital a little past four and

Lily is waiting in the turn-about where the ambulances park to rush patients inside. She's got a cast on her right wrist and she brightens when she sees me, then climbs into the truck between Daniel and I. He asks her what had happened and Lily insists she fell wrong while playing volleyball and tells the story convincingly. I hardly notice that Daniel has turned us off the main road early, going east for a while on a muddy trail with branches draped low over it. I know this trail, though I never traveled it by car. He says he wants to show us something that he's been working on, and my reaction is informed by Lily's, and she looks at ease. But I recognize the waters of Little Bass a mile off with the treeline reflected on the water, and soon, the Cottonwood dead at its heights on the Promontory. Lily is unfazed looking at it all through the windows. She knows but lets nothing show. "There's a nice place for a dock," says Daniel of the headland. "Don't you think?"

"You can do that?"

"Why not? It's state land now, but I figure if they won't give me my dues I'll just take them."

The sky darkens with overcast. The truck labors over deadwood littered over the forgotten road. Much of it has been pulled to the side, and what's left has been trampled and mashed to mulch by the tires. The road ends at the steps of the boathouse standing on stilts, black against the water.

"What is this place?" asks Lily. But she knows. The boathouse is visible from across the water, hidden under the shadows of ash trees. Neither of us could have imagined that her father had taken residence here, and I think we're both stricken with the thought that he might have seen us coming and going from the Promontory all this time.

"I found it by accident," claims Daniel. "There's something with that place, that house of your mother's. It makes us crazy. But we can get away once in a while. Get your mother off that sofa. I think it would be good for us to come here sometimes. Together or not together. You see that cliff across the lake with the big tree? That's an Eastern Cottonwood. It goes up a hundred feet. People used to camp there for the view, not really to enjoy it, but because it offered protection from animals and other people. But we can just enjoy it for the view," he says with a gaunt smile. It has the feeling of a strange man stepping uninvited into a child's fort. Lily tries for a smile too, tries to look happy but there is no happiness. In regard to her parents she has nothing but fear toward them anymore. It isn't that house. It's them. They'll poison this place as they do every other place. Their voices will carry easily over the water. The croaking from her mother that picks at the weakest parts of things and of people. Her father's anger and his strange desperation. Lily looks around to the lake and the Promontory as if for the last time. *It's okay,* I will tell her when I can. *We'll find someplace else.*

Daniel steps out from the truck. He brought a standing lamp and a little side table from their home and tells me to help him. I grab the lamp from the back of the truck draped over with tarp and bring it inside. "By the loveseat," he says, motioning with his head. I stand it there and plug the cord into a nearby outlet and pull the chain but it doesn't come on.

"There hasn't been a working power line here in ten years," says Daniel. "I'll have to wire the place to a generator if we're gonna have any electricity. I don't suppose you have any experience in that?" I shake my head and he laughs and says, "Well what can you do?" I look around unsure. Lily is out by the water, peering into it and lost in her own thoughts "Can you lay wood? Hammer nails?" asks Daniel. I shrug. "Or do you think I'll keep letting you hang around my daughter for free?"

"I can help," I say.

"Good. Just don't tell anyone you're helping me out here, alright? Nobody but the two of you knows about this place, so if authorities come by one day to kick me out of here I'll know exactly who to blame," he says. I nod.

We bring a couple more things inside from his truck. Boxes of kitchen stuff, I think. When we're finished Daniel closes up the bed of the truck and goes inside, leaving the front door to the boathouse open. I've got my Polaroid with me in my backpack. I take it out and snap a picture, and when the photo rolls out I stuff it and the camera back into my backpack.

Daniel calls for us to come inside and to close the door. He's excited to show us his progress. The lower floor where a small boat would have dock and tied has been boarded up with used wood and turned into a living space. It was simple enough to turn the upper floor into two bedrooms, and it even has a bathroom, but no shower. Lily's eyes keep falling on the shore across the lake though every window that offers a view of it, like she's taking note of what can be seen from here. The answer is that all of it can.

There's a shallow stream nearby – a light dulcet of clean and cold water. It takes the cadence of speech. I make my way into the stream with the cold water seeping into my boots, kneel, and drink. Pure as glacial ice melt. Then I stand, too quickly, clutching my head against the onset of vertigo. When it passes I follow the stream and come to a rise of slippery rocks with the stream flowing down in veins between them. I climb and at the top are swirling riffle pools into which the rivulets flow from the east, uttering their strange words: "Shell. Sun. There. Hush."

Foxtail against my fingers. A gust of wind passing through them. The vertigo returns. I sit for as long as it takes to pass, head down on my arms. The sun is out and coming off the water to heat my face.

Off the edge of the boat and down in the sandy water I can just make out the dark spine of the walleye piking its way through a forest of lakeweed. "I'd like to meet her parents," says Dad.

"You've talked to them on the phone before. I've listened to you," I say.

"That's not the same."

I shrug and push the hook through the wreathing black leech and lower it into the water, right over the walleye.

"Is that alright?" he asks.

"She isn't my girlfriend or anything."

"That doesn't matter."

"Why don't you want to meet Hakon's parents?"

Dad looks at me, then down at his hands that hold his own leech, but it wriggles free and falls into the boat somewhere. He grabs another from the styrofoam cup and hooks it. "She's so much like you were." He says, then he asks if I remember how I was when he and Mom were fighting.

"No," I say. "How was I?"

"You stopped talking to us. You used to tell us everything, even about your dreams and your nightmares, but then you didn't tell us anything at all."

"I don't tell you about my dreams now."

"You're too old now," he says with a little smile, and with a subtle flick of his wrists the fishing rod lashes out a figure eight above him and the line is flung a surprising distance near a patch of lily pads by the shore.

"It's just, we're supposed to dream of things important to us, but I dream of nothing important to anyone," I say. The walleye that was orbiting my line is gone. "Maybe when dreams are all that's left to see, I'll tell you about them then."

The smile on his face vanishes, and the bloodless white creases around his eyes fill with color again. "It's Lily's birthday in a month," he says. "I think we should plan for something. Have you got her anything?"

"It's her birthday?"

"You don't know when her birthday is?"

"I never asked."

"You need to know these things, son. She knows

yours. She knows everything about you."

"How do you know she knows everything about me?"

"I just do. Get her something. I'll give you money."

"Like what?"

"Don't you know her at all? Think of something. You have to do this, okay?"

"Alright."

The light is unusually calm, and it's darker than it has been in a long time. "Can we have a fire?" I ask.

"It isn't cold," says Mom.

"But it's storming out," I say. Through the window lightning crawls across the sky and rain taps the glass.

"Alright," she says. I pile on the logs and stuff old newspapers under them and Mom lights it up with a match. We turn the lights out so it's just the fire and lightning flapping together in the dark. I sit in the rocking chair and Mom sits in one of the slipper chairs. "Did you get her anything yet?" she asks.

"Yes."

"Something real? Not a gag, or something thoughtless?"

"Something real, I think." In the dark Mom folds her arms. "Something that's a shared interest of ours, but I'm not sure how much she's interested or if she's just pretending."

"Why do you think that?"

"Because I'm pretending. A little."

"Can I see it?"

I stand from the rocking chair and go into my room and grab the present from my drawer and give it to her in the living room. She weighs it in her hand. "It's heavy. Where do you get a thing like this anyway?"

"Dad took me into Ely. There's an arts and crafts store and we talked to a lady there and she got it for us. It took two weeks."

"How much was it?"

"I'm not sure."

Mom smiles. "I think she'll love it. I love it. I can't wait to see her face when you give it to her." She sets it down on the little table between the slipper chairs. "Have you asked her what she wants to do for her birthday?"

"No."

"You don't like the idea?"

"It's not that. Her mom doesn't like me. Her dad barely does. I don't go to her house very often anymore." Of course, I go there all the time helping Daniel, but I'm careful not to let that slip.

"What are they like?"

"They hate each other," I say.

"That's all?"

"It's hard to notice anything else... I've never seen her mom off the sofa. Her dad is drunk a lot of the time. They argue, but I've never heard them involve Lily. Not ever."

"What does Lily say?"

"She wishes they would separate. She thinks they will very soon. I asked her who she would go with if they did, and she said her mom, but only because she wouldn't have to move away. And then she said that since I'm moving anyway, it doesn't matter who she goes with." Mom goes quiet for a time. She and Dad decided months ago we would leave for the city, for my sake, and I suspect it was a stipulation for them to stay together. I watch her the best I can about my peripherals, around the luminous green-white eye that comes to stare at me in the dark like something of another world encroaching on ours, manifesting in front of my face. I look into the fire to what of it can be seen through the bright iris to as if to remind the eyes to peer past it. That always helps a little.

Mom reaches over to the side table and picks up the resin dome again and brings it to her belly and watches it in the light of the fire and lightning. "It's important we meet them, Avery. I think you should try to spend her birthday there. We'll swing by to pick you up and to introduce ourselves. Is that alright?"

I nod to her in the darkness. "Okay."

There are sirens far in the distance. A tandem of emergency vehicles joins in with the chatter of two helicopters circling the area where I lit the fire. I can smell it on the wind. More than just wood smoke. It seems the whole place went up. I don't think it was me, and I heard a shot awhile back too. Maybe the soul goes on where the body cannot. I can't remember the last time I felt any pain. Even when I press on the wound near my neck there's nothing. I think to stand but then I think it would be better stay. The cold of the water is meaningless now, and there's comfort in the thought of being pulled back into the earth, safe at last. Nothing will find me there.

Then again, this is all only half to do with me.

I stand and my head spins and I wait there in the shallow riffle pools for it to pass. The blades of a distant helicopters resonate with the throbbing in my head, amplifying it until the vibration can be seen again. Really *seen*. It won't go away, not in time, so I move on despite it, going against the flow of the water.

The whole sky seems to tremble, the sounds of the airshow far to the southeast over Ely ricochet all around us. Sometimes jets pass over in pairs, making too much noise for their size and distance. F-16s I think. I can hardly make them out anymore. Lily is looking up at them through the trees and she turns to me and asks if I can see them too. I shrug at her, as always.

The resin dome swags heavily in my sweater pocket. I thought to wait for her birthday in a couple weeks but with her parents there it would be like passing her contraband through a cell rather than giving her a gift. I take it from my pocket and give it a final appraisal in the golden light of the low sun, bringing it close to my eyes to see the architecture of the wings magnified some through the resin, and all else that's legible in the numerations of scales and colors. A world of detail is contained here. Any picture, any story ever told. I rub it clean of fingerprints with the sleeve of my sweater. "Lily?"

She turns, her arms swinging out like the hem of

her dress. Her eyes fall to the Cecropia in my hands and I hold it out to her. "For your birthday," I say, embarrassed. I've never given anyone a gift before. She folds into herself, shy at first, then sad and then happy, opening again. She takes it in her hands and peers into it as I did. Her hair is brighter in the sun than the light of blindness. Her face is so pale.

"Thank you," she says.

I smile fleetingly. "Since I couldn't find one myself. And, even if I did, they're so fragile and they die so fast..."

"It's perfect. She looks alive. Doesn't she?" Lily holds it in her palms like it should take flight.

"She does."

Another wing of jets pass over. I crane my head up to catch the sight of them. Four F-18s this time, but I can't be sure. There's a pattern of orange clouds strung up on their contrails, and the shadows of the jets are projected onto the underside of the clouds far behind the formation. Then, I lose them against the sky. If things continue as they have that was the last I'll ever see.

Lily steps in close. Slow but unexpected. She's holding her breath and there's concern in her eyes, where everything described of the Cecropia is true for them as well. Far from her I forget how small she is, and how light. Here where the pine go up straight and narrow as the feathers of pheasants she takes my hand and kisses me for the first time. So soft I hardly feel it, like falling to bed. Such a small and brief sensation, it's like it never happened at all. A short reprieve then it's gone. Only seconds have passed and already the longing after its absence is worse than any pleasure there was when it arrived. A novel kind of torture.

Stop there. Do not go on. You may die soon to reiterate through your life, those moments forever, and that makes each its own eternity. Go back and stay.

Death back there.

Death ahead of you. Stay where it's warm.

It isn't warm.

Dream then. You were, moments ago. Please.

I've tried, but it moves uncannily. The memory does not.

"Why did you do that?" I ask her.

Her eyes drift open. "I don't know," she says, looking down at her feet. "I thought I should."

We walk on. Those unseen aircraft grouse and carve up the sky and then the show is done. The skies above Ely are quiet again. Lily patiently follows behind without a word. I stumble, unable to make out the twist of roots at my feet. She's watching me. "If I ask you something will you tell me the truth?" I say.

"Yes, I will," she says.

"What if it's something you're embarrassed about?"

"I will."

We go across the glulam bridge, the amber creek running shallowly with the smell of decaying fish wafting from it. "What if it's something you're guilty about?"

"Yes, Avery," she says with a flurry of laughter like there's nothing she could be guilty about.

"Have you told anyone I was going blind? Did you tell that kid?"

She stops. So do I. "What kid? No, I couldn't have."

"How did he know about it?"

"Maybe he heard it from someone else. Hakon could have told him."

"I never told Hakon about it. Did you?"

"I've never told anyone."

"But I've only told you. So how did he know?" I'm careful not to sound angry, but I am angry and she probably knows it.

"You must have said something and you just don't remember," she says.

I turn to her. Her head is tilted to the side and her hair covers part of her face and she's looking up at me through the curtains of her bangs. It's the look she gave me when we first met. "I would remember if I told someone," I say.

"So would I," she whispers.

"He said you told him, and he knew. What should I think about that?"

"Why would I tell him? I hardly know him."

"You told him because you're worried."

"About what?"

"About what would happen if you had to lead me around all the time. Maybe you told him because it's in the back of your mind all the time."

"It isn't."

"Of course it is."

"No, it isn't."

"Maybe not consciously, but it's there. How can't it be?"

She looks down at her hands gripping the Cecropia, concealing it, like I'm going to take it back from her. "Do you think about how small, or how pale I am all the time?"

"Those things don't matter."

"And none of your things matter."

"But you talk to other people about them."

"I told you I didn't tell anyone."

"Then you're lying."

"I'm not! I just…"

Her voice catches. She cannot go on and folds into herself, shrinking smaller and smaller as she does so often. Only this time, she doesn't return as she was, doesn't open up again. All progress bringing her out into the world gone in an instant. She can't speak anymore. There's no breath long enough to allow it between choked sobs. But she doesn't cry for long. The woods are too quiet and she won't weep into the silence for it to carry far. Lily composes herself and is changed. Somehow I understand that I'll never see her like that again. I've become untrustworthy. Another of dozens to guard her feelings against. The look she gives now is new on her but I recognize it anyway. I've seen it on myself peering into the mirror and trying to imagine and put to memory what I might look like older. What it must mean is that she now keeps behind her heart some negation of any good she sees. The eventuality of things;

the truth about me. "Just forget about it," I say, but Lily won't forget and neither will I.

She has no grave, but her ashes were scattered in the rivers near her mother's home. I would address those of them gathered here: We should have been better matched to our environments. It would have been less tragic if it had been me there in your place.

Or, is it possible you're alive somehow? Remembered in perfect detail, does the memory of a person become sentient? A bicameral being sharing one mind? If that's true then you know I thought to say I'm sorry. I'm sure I thought to do it... it's hard to remember. Hindsight influences the recollection. I'm a separate person narrating the past experiences and thoughts of another. Still, I'm certain I knew it was silly of me to accuse you of anything. It didn't matter if you told anyone.

God, take me back there. I'll happily die here and chase the soul to hell and torment it myself if it means going back. I'll take her and run. I swear to you.

There's no bargaining. The math works against you. You're outnumbered by things set in motion long before you were born and they have all the momentum behind them and there is none of it behind you. She was going to say that she loved you but never could. Or would you do harm to her memory? Now think. You didn't catch her in a lie. Her actions don't lend to guilt. It was Daniel who told. He must have learned it through your parents. He must have set that kid, Frank, against you in some game of his. And Daniel did to him what he tried to do to you, only you had run and Frank took to killing. It's that kid who hunts you, now grown. What was it said to you near Giant's Tooth and then on Twin Bridge? Yes, you remember. Now go. You've just arrived and it's time to end all this.

Listen. Something skirts the water's surface. Loons lifting into the air. It's Little Bass Lake. You're there. Go north along its shore for a half-mile to a span of beachfront where a strange silence waits. You remember. It's a berm of dead willow, their naked branches uttering nothing of the breeze passing through them. Daniel chose them for their significance and to remember the place from the land.

The boathouse was almost complete and he'd asked for my help clearing waste. We'd all gone there that day, even the mother was taken from her couch and sat in the back of the crew cab mute and catatonic like a drugged asylum patient. It was overcast that day, the clouds as dark and definite as the ocean. Lily had her head rested against the passenger window, saying nothing.

We drive up to the porch, the front passenger tire pressing against the first step. I figure Daniel might be drunk on the medicine again. Lily climbs out as soon as he puts the truck in park and she leads her mother inside by the hand. Daniel, meanwhile, asks for me to come with him and I agree, and we go a mile or so to the south in his truck, keeping mostly to the shoreline of Little Bass. We stop and he climbs out and pads over to the rear and I follow him there. He opens the bed and black water spills out onto our shoes. It smells like oil and roadkill. Daniel pulls at a heavy jute sack. "Get that end," he tells me.

I grab hold and we slide it from the bed. Its contents fold over my arms. "What's in it?" I ask.

"Carrion," he says. "I don't want it near the boathouse to attract bears." We carry the jute sack to a willow tree where he started a small hole. "Let's leave it here," he says, and we drop it and he fetches some shovels out the truck bed and hands one to me and we dig the hole further down into the red then black clay. Water fills in at the bottom. We dig a little past the water line then Daniel throws down his shovel and goes back to his truck and gets two amber glass bottles from a cooler; a beer for himself and a coke for me. We're filthy and tired and we rest awhile and drink. When recouped we return to the hole and drag the stinking sack into it. Daniel starts to shovel wet pats of clay into it right away. I take up my shovel and do likewise, the mud sucking at the back of the spade and slapping down onto the jut sack in the hole. The two of us work into a rhythm, my shovel than his, conveying mud into the dark and red excavation like packing the cone of an amputated limb with gauze, and the jut sack down there like the pale bone. And it seems there are exactly these things down there. Though it's difficult to make them out, I have to squint to be sure, but when Daniel tosses another cut of clay onto the sack it presses the material down taught around the form of a howling mouth, an oval over which the latticed threads hang like the web of some terrible arachnid, and above it is a triangle for the nose and two round sockets for the eyes. I don't really trust what I see down there, and I go on shoveling, but the form of that howling face doesn't go away like a thing seen in the shadows in my peripherals. It's there. It always has been, and when it can no longer be ignored I stare long into the eyes, straining to see past the light and moving the obscured focal of my vision around it so there's no mistake. Yes, there it is.

I can't move even though I want to. Daniel is whistling the cadence of our work before he notices that I've stopped moving. At the fringes of my vision I see his face turn up to me. My clothes are damp with the dark water which had steeped in the decaying flesh down there for God knows how long. The stench of it becomes intolerable for knowing what it is. "What's wrong?" asks Daniel, like he doesn't know it's down there. I can't speak, and without thinking, I'm holding the shovel as a weapon against the man.

"What? That?" he motions with his shovel into the grave. "I've been meaning to tell you. I guess I thought you knew about it. Either way, you just helped me. We're together in this now. So just dig, alright?" He goes back to shoveling clay into the grave. I can't, though. I'm all seized up like the corpse down there. Each cut of earth mercifully blots the sight of it, but it remains there like everything else remains, bright as the moment first seen. "Go on, dig," he says.

The grave is filled with clay now, but Daniel and I never finished burying the body ourselves. At this time I no longer doubt what I remember, so the simple answer is that it was filled through erosion over the years, or it was filled by somebody else. Frank? Maybe. A question for another time.

Daniel must see it on my face that I won't go on helping him. "Okay. That's alright," he says. "I'll drive you back to your house if you agree never to talk about this." I step back from him, the mud pulling at my shoes. "Come on, let's go." He holds out his hand for me to take, the other cocked back and holding the spade. "Don't make me chase you, boy," he says. My foot sinks deep into the mud and I fall on my back. Daniel rushes me, but I'm quick to get on my feet again and retreat just inches from his grasp. He falls where I fell in the mud, and enfeebled by old injuries, he can't stand quick enough before I dart into the surrounding woods and run until his shrieking becomes distant, then falls silent. I hunker behind the shroud of an alder bush, peering through it. Daniel has climbed into his truck. The engine jumps up and he whips it around, the headlights panning into the darkening forest and over me and I go to the ground. His eyes are keen and the engine barks and the truck charges forward. I dash into a dense patch of oak and hold there. The truck slides to a halt before them and he climbs out with a rifle in his hands, scanning the copse I hide. For a moment it looks like he sees me and I almost burst from hiding to make a run for it, but his gaze crawls over me and over the foliage at my sides. He fires a shot from the hip and I remain still. "I won't bother chasing you!" he shouts. Then he puts the rifle over his back and rests his slender and sagging arms over it like through a pillory. "You know where to find me. You know exactly where I'll go now, and what I have to do, don't you? But if you come out it'll just be you and that'll be the end of it. Your choice."

I don't move. I believe him and I don't move.

"Did you hear me?" He rocks back and forth with the rifle over his shoulders. Even with the light he is clearly seen, and if he stands there much longer he'll surely see me hiding here. "Look, I'll put the rifle down. There." He does and splays his arms. "We can fight, okay? Whoever loses will join the man in that hole back there. If it's you, you'll have to hide me like I'll have to hide you, because there won't be any way to separate your deeds from mine. You'll see. So how about it?" He waits only a moment then he sneers and snatches the rifle from the mud and climbs back into the truck. It whips around again and peels off sending twin arks of mud into the air, fishtailing along the shoreline back toward the boathouse.

There was no going for help. I knew what he meant. Maybe he'd planned it a long time ago and maybe not. Before my wits could convince me otherwise I followed him as fast as I could back for two miles of lakefront until I came to the sound of waves glancing off the stilts of the boathouse in the water. It was totally dark by the time I arrived, and I've held onto the sounds of things as much as what I saw. There was commotion inside. I meant to get her out of there.

Aaron

He's holding the photo at me. My own reflection distorted on its surface and shaking with a slight tremor of his hand. "I have nothing for you," I tell him.

"Not even a guess? A man's life is on the line," says Sean.

"There are a hundred places like that around here. It would be by sheer luck to guess it right."

"Then let it be by luck."

"We haven't got any."

"William took this picture."

"He did."

"You knew him. He and your brother's daughter were inseparable."

"What are you saying?"

"I'm saying I find it unlikely you weren't aware that your brother claimed himself another home. I'm saying we can solve his murder and find William at the same time, and that if I were you, I'd order every lakefront in a twenty mile radius scrutinized until this place is found," he says. And he's right. Anything less than that suggests either corruption or profound incompetence. Besides, the boathouse will be found eventually, and William is probably dead. Why not give it to him?

I take the photo from his hands and make a show of studying it more closely. "It has to be near his home," I say. Sean folds his arms. "Either Bushmen Lake, east of it, or Little Bass to the west."

A Beacon in the Light

William

Daniel's truck idles in the driveway. Its front tires are mounted over the landing board of the stoop. The door is open. No one inside. The rifle isn't there either. I go to the bed of the truck and take up a felling ax and enter through the half-open doorway of the boathouse. A light is on but the shadows are all cast at uncanny angles. The standing lamp has been dashed to the ground and its shade is gone. The harsh shadows glow a little with dim cold light from another source – a small television turned to static that pops and foams through the speakers. The armrest of the loveseat is slashed open and there's pink in the white cotton. Shattered dishes on the wood floor boards everywhere. Shouting upstairs, Daniel and Emily. Lily is talking between them. I can't hear the words, but she sounds strangely calm. I want to rush upstairs but I can hardly move at all.

I walked as though on stilts, and I go so now. It was fear then but presently the wood is unstable under my feet, untended and rotting in the damp all these years.

The stairs are dotted with blood, a line of it ascending all the way to the top. Lily has gone quiet now. It's just Daniel and Emily shouting words I don't really hear. My legs are like rebar, and it's a great effort to move them, but I reach the top of the steps and go to the room that falls silent as I turn the corner. There, the man and the woman are holding each other in the dark. It's unclear at first who's bleeding between them, but there's a lot of it in their clothes and about their arms. Lily is sitting in a wooden chair looking no more dismayed than if she had been placed in time-out. On her face is a look of mild frustration. She watches them like they could be discussing her grades. When Lily sees me in the doorway she gets to her feet, and I hold my hand out to her. She means to leave with me, that moment playing out as it did so many times before when we would make a quick get-away together, but she can't now. Something's wrong. A dark spot of blood shows through her white nightgown, no larger than a fingerprint. She does not take my hand, but walks past me like I'm not there and wanders into another room. Daniel sees, and sees me there at the entrance with the ax held against the both of them. I know Daniel is a murderer, but for me, both of them stand against us; the two united only for this moment, but that's long enough. They're the same. Maybe that's not right but I don't care. I'll make sure that was the last they'll see of Lily ever again.

Daniel doesn't have the rifle anymore, but a carving knife instead. I think to go find it but then I think doing that would leave Lily unguarded. I have to stay.

They separate from one another and look at each other, at the wounds they've inflicted. The mother, with her scrawny body pressing through her white gown and the bones of her face pressing through the skin, turns and takes a step in some effort to confront me. I bring the ax up, but Daniel grabs her dark hair and yanks her head back and slides the knife deep into her neck.

"There," he says into her ear. "How's that?" He forces her to look at him. "How was that?" he says to her face. Her mouth drops into a black oval and her arms reach out, grasping at nothing, letting the blood flow freely from her neck. Daniel lets go of her and she stumbles back and turns. They look at one another again, Emily with her slack face and the warm rope of blood running down to the floor, and him with eyes calm and menacing. The blade in his hand shines red and the refraction off its edge does not shake. His hands are perfectly still. "Sit down on that bed," he says to her. She obeys, moving there and plopping down, then she looks up at him for more instruction. In her final moments she's the dutiful wife at last. "Lie down," he commands, and she does. "Just wait for me there, okay?" Emily nods, the movement opening and closing the fatal wound in her neck. Her black eyes fall on me then. Daniel's too, and the spectacle playing out on the other side of the room reaches out to touch its lone audience member, like some fiendish circus act. "Put that ax down," says Daniel, very tired all of a sudden. The woman on the bed spasms, her entire body seized by one last critical burst of adrenaline and it occurs to her at last to keep the blood in. But it's too late, and her arms curl up and she trembles violently before going limp, then she sags into the maroon soaked sheets and is gone. "Go on, put it down, it's over. I'm done, okay?" He says this in a tone removed from what's happened, like he's had some meaningless argument. He's concealing the blade behind his thigh and approaches me with his empty hand held out pleadingly. I swing the ax at him, the weight of it throwing me off balance but the moment is too brief for him to use, though he brings the blade out anyway. There's no hiding his intent now, and he gets in a stance that speaks of experience in fighting with a blade. "It's too late to find your balls, kid. What does having that ax change? You should have come from hiding if you wanted a fight. It would have only been you then, do you understand that?"

I raise the ax above my head. I'll get one shot. The moment I commit to a blow and miss he'll tangle me up and slide that blade across my throat. I have enough experience in fighting to know that at least. He knows too, and tries to coax a swing out of me several times, feigning a charge or swiping the blade out benignly. He mistakes me for being totally helpless. He thinks I'm dead already. It's something about my face. Hakon says I look scared when I fight even though I fight too often to be scared. He says it gives me some advantage, since I look harmless and people think they can just come at me and I won't know what to do. I've learned to play into it too, to play the coward who can't fight. My shoulders go slack and my arms buckle inward like I've been taken with fear. The display of weakness seems to amuse Daniel, and he comes in with the blade held lightly in his hand. It catches the moonlight like a banner of neon as he lashes it out to me. I put everything into the falling blow. My core and the strength of my arms and the weight of my body pressing the axhead down through the air and it arcs square onto the man's knife hand, splitting it between the middle and ring finger. Just a crab claw now.

He yelps and jerks his arm away then collapses around the ruined hand, clutching at it with his good one. I have it in me to kill him right there.

<u>Frank</u>

Rings of moonlight gleam on the fringes of his footprints. We follow as fast as we can up an acclivity of slippery rocks where a stream runs through. Glen is close behind, breathing heavily with the effort to keep up. When the ground levels out I spot a length of sliding footprints on the mossy rims of the tepid riffle pools. Our stride is twice that of his.

In some minutes we come to a lakefront with the stars reflected at our feet. The footprints track north and we follow them to a boathouse. The boathouse. One of its stilts gave out a long time ago and half the rear deck is sunken in the water. I'm guessing the man plans to spring an ambush inside, so I signal Glen for silence and we glide to the half-sunken structure, stepping onto the porch, kneeling to listen. Inside is total silence, like a presence hushes the critters that might otherwise make themselves known; like something in there presses down on the woodworks that might otherwise stir in the wind. He's waiting for us. Glen checks his rifle one last time and gives me a nod.

Daniel tries to stand from the floor but he slips on the woman's blood dripping from the bed. I bring the ax down on his shin at a bad angle, the axhead glancing off, but the force of it shattering his bone. He screams. I swing again at his legs and miss and kerf the cedar boards. Again, and the axhead passes right through his foot, deadening the toes. He yelps on every blow, even the ones that don't land, and he bargains between each one. He says he's finished and he's sorry and I can stop now. But I won't. It only angers me.

He gives up on begging and crawls to the door of the bedroom, dragging his mangled legs behind him with a streak of blood following. He calls out for Lily. I hear it between heartbeats, and that decides it for me. I'm going to kill him.

He throws himself down the narrow stairs then lifts himself upright with help from the newel post and goes for the landing door. His hands are coated with blood and they slip over the brass knob uselessly. I rush down at him and strike the hand groping at the door, severing two fingers. He looks at them on the floor and looks at the fountains of crimson from the stumps on his hand like the pain of it is trivial by now. I raise the ax again and bring it down onto his skull. He doesn't go down at once, but I know it's done. I felt it in the handle. There's no surviving that blow. He's able to open the door at last and he stumbles outside but doesn't get far. All the life goes from him suddenly, and he collapses in the wet silt like a marionette cut from its strings, and is still. I watch him there, to be sure. The tension and strength in my hands expiring a fiber at a time like a rope bearing too much weight and fraying apart. When there's no strength left to hold anything in them the ax falls to the floor. The sound it makes is like a knock at the door; a utensil clattering onto the table top, or a glass set upon it. The sounds of that struggle like the whisper of traffic far away or the sigh of someone sleeping close; like a sharp breath, or the wind. The delta of blood that ran down the woman's gown onto the floor, like soapy shower water on the tile, or like rain in the summer when the drops are warm and heavy. I know that from now on any sight or sound that bears resemblance to what was seen and heard here is adulterated forever.

When I could move again, I climbed the stairs and found Lily in the small room she had retreated to, underneath a bed pushed to the corner. She had pulled down the white blanket with her, where she'd tucked herself away like an animal ready to die. I laid on the floor, right here at my feet. Her face was hardly a shade darker than the blanket. Her fingers gripped a tuft of fabric held over her mouth. She looked frightened, and said something but I couldn't hear what, her voice remembered now as a static-brittle sibilance at the very limits of some seeking instrument. She let go from the white blanket and held her hand out for me to take, but I was afraid. I understood it as some final act that would send her off. But, in one last effort of bravery, I did take her hand. Thank God, and she was okay. On her face was something like contemplation. It was the face she'd make when it was time for me to take her away through any door unobserved, and we'd run until there was enough forest to blot the sight of any place there were people.

Frank

A sudden commotion stirs the silence inside. Footfalls coming swiftly down the stairs on the far side of the main room. I hurry inside but get only a glimpse of the man going through the landing door. I rush around the patio and take aim with my rifle into the darkness and fire at a shadow briefly blotting the reflected stars on the water. Glen runs up from behind me and shines his light at the fleeing man but by then he's gone into the trees and they send the light back into our eyes. "Turn it off!" I say, and he does, but the harm is done. My vision is obscured now and I can't see the man dashing into the woods just meters away!

We set off after him but he's gained a surprising distance from us in the pitch of night. It's like he isn't impeded at all by the foliage and uncertain ground. The trees grab at my arms and legs and every open way between them leads to some tangle of brambles and leaves and branches. I press through, carefully, as not to cut myself or to leave anything to be found later. I stop in a small clearing and brace the butt of my rifle against my hip and fire into the dark toward the sound of the man rushing through the trees, but he goes on. It occurs to me I'd never really seen him, not once a good look. Always far off like a shadow, and it must be true for him as well.

Glen catches up to me, heaving. "You sure it's not some animal?" he says.

"I'm sure."

"You saw him?"

"Just follow. He can't have much left."

William

I ran down the narrow beach into the trees. Their limbs tore at my face and it's so now. I'm bigger than I was but I don't need to move as I did or risk losing my way. There's little else so remembered as the way from here to the Promontory. We walked these edge-waters a hundred times. All of it justified in place and time here. All of it as it was.

I ran like the exhaustion would blot out any thoughts of what had happened. Like it would make thinking impossible beyond the pain. I was right, and ran until my lungs were raw and my legs burned and no thought could penetrate through. I went into a thicket of ash saplings and became lost, and for a while, abandoned any notion of a direction, but I kept moving out of fear of being still. Sooner than I had then, I find the water through an expanse of tall grass and I go into the shallow waves. Deepening, swimming now through reeds.

Frank

In the dark comes the crash of forded water. I push through the dense brush toward the sound and soon emerge onto the lapping edge of Little Bass. Glen ignites his light again and pans it over the surface but there's nothing but a flock of loons huddled near the water's edge and they sputter and skirt in unison from the light, and from something else in the water. I shoot one of them in the neck. It splays its wings to take flight, flapping without effect, then it sinks into the blackness. The others take off in all directions but nothing is revealed in the water. I shine my own light at the shore to our left and right and into the reeds but there's no sign of him. He must be in the lake, but the waves are just high enough to conceal him breaking out of the surface for air. Glen fires his own rifle, the bullet carving into the water and spalling into shards harmless as hailstones that scatter across the lake beyond our lights. It won't work to panic the man. Even cowards become numb to fright after so much of it. "We'll go around," I say. "He'll be too tired to get far from the shore."

"It's miles around," he says. "What if he turns back?"

"He won't turn back."

"You don't know what he'll do." His eyes search the darkness ahead.

"Go north," I tell him. "I'll go south. One of us has to pick up his trail."

He looks at me, making no attempt at hiding his

suspicions. The man's most defining feature is a deep groove in his forehead when he went through a windshield a long time ago. The scar is obvious even in the shadows. He has no hope at all. "You think he never saw you but you don't know that for sure," he says to me.

"No, I don't know that for sure."

He points his light at my feet to see me better, making a shadow of himself and of his eyes. "Alright," he says. "I'll see you on the other side."

I nod to him and we part, myself going south and he to the north.

William

I wade under the surface, turning onto my back and taking air into my lungs. I nearly drowned then. The distance from the eastern shore and the Promontory is greater than the eye can tell and I hardly reached the other side before my arms gave out. But I am not as panicked as I was. Though hindered some by the wound near my neck, there are no currents strong enough to push against me or to carry me off course and I make steady progress. The water is mild. There's nothing in the lake to give evidence of its depths but the depths are there. Four-hundred feet in some places where a thing can remain untouched for thousands of years. Like in a dream I don't tire, and soon, the reeds by the shoreline brush against my hands. They come up from a deep tunnel of amber water like the tails of kites drifting down from the sky. I run aground, my fingers clawing the slippery surface of algae-coated granite, and I stand, falling many times, and climb the headland. I collapse at the bole of the great Cottonwood. I was crying, couldn't stop.

The roots are strong. The wood is healthy and the leaves hush in the wind. It's quiet all around me. Breathe. It's only you here.

Like this place, I went anywhere difficult to find or to reach. In such places it guarantees that those most like myself would be there and those most unlike me would not. In the city it became the rooftops or the heights of its walls. I was alone often, but there would be others there too sometimes. Jessica asked once, when we first met, if I'd come to the top of the mountain at night for the city lights as she had. She said without the stars they do just as well.

The way ends here. It's far enough I think.

Aaron

The call comes ten till five in the morning. The boathouse has been located, and very near it are shell casings and some tracks that police are making slow progress following. They were there, that much is known. If William isn't dead already then they're right behind him. Seconds behind him.

Sean and I await update in silence. There's nothing left for me on my desk to occupy the hands and eyes so I turn from him to the window behind, and against the gray sky there's a Cessna flying slowly over the black trees and squat buildings like it should stall, but it doesn't. A headwind keeps it up there, and if it turns away it could stall, so it can't.

If I've devised a hundred ways to lie then I have a thousand to tell the truth. But each of those are self-deceptions too. All that can be said for sure is that Daniel called me one day crying. He told me he'd killed someone in self-defense but it didn't look like it at all. He was right. It looked like murder, and there was no way to make it look another way. I helped him hide what he'd done anyway. Why? Unknowable. I'm too many at the controls. Another had them and bailed and now it's just me keeping things up. Why bother anymore? I turn to Sean; just a shadow in the pale of the early morning through the window, but there's enough to light the white crescents of his eyes and they do not move for a long time. "I know where William is going," I tell him, feeling weightless when I do.

His eyes shift. "You do?"

"Yes."

Warnings. Red lights. Final attempts by the multitudes to keep it all precariously aloft by some means. The weight of it comes back even at the thought. I don't want it on me anymore. Besides I couldn't do it then and can't do it now. "There's a promontory on the western shore of Little Bass," I say. "A big cottonwood tree like you see in paintings. He'll be there."

The man shakes his head. "How do you figure that?"

He doesn't know when to quit. "Because that's

where I found him the last time."

William

The apparition of the Milky Way swung over the trees. It was September then, the sky should look only a little bit different. The dim crown of it passed behind the stem of the Cottonwood and then it passed the horizon. A loon called sometimes. I laid here for three days and on the final morning emerged a teal sky in the east. When the leaves were lit by the sun they were like fire, and I wanted the blindness to come then and for that to persist forever and nothing else. But a shadow came over me. For a long time a man stood there. "Oh God. Oh Christ," he said and wept from a deep lode of despair, and spoke names as though to etch them onto headstones placed there and forgotten. The man left me but hours later returned and told me that everything would be okay, a promise like some final resolution after lengthy bargaining.

I was taken from the ground and in some elision of dreams and shadows I woke up in the hospital. My father was there. I tried to speak but I could only cry. After a long time he explained that I was found near Burntside not a mile from our home. I sat bewildered as he told me that Lily, Daniel and Emily had also been found near Burntside, only a mile from where I was.

My father asked what had happened, what I had seen, but I couldn't lie to him. I couldn't tell him what I thought had to be wrong, and for the first time I saw him cry. "It's okay," he said, and he held me to him. "I won't force anything from you. But when you have it right, you have to tell us what happened. Okay? Please son." I promised him and he never asked me about it again. He must have died afraid I would never be okay.

Jessica is here now. She asks if I can hear her, and it's easy to pick her voice out from the din of doctors calling for medication and police making way ahead. She's in no panic at all, and with that, the pain is gone, or becomes the kind that makes you better. A needle slides into my arm and then there's the taste of salt from the saline. She stays for a long time speaking often in my ear.

Hours or days pass. I can't be sure which.

The doctor is called in. He asks if I know where I am. Whispers and conversation. Jessica is taken from the room but she tells me she'll be right back. A new voice says, "The man himself," and waits for an answer but I can't just yet. "The doctor said you were responsive, but if you don't want to talk now I can come back later."

"I can talk now," I manage.

He slides a metal chair over the linoleum near to my gurney. "Good. It's urgent." The click of a pen and reticulation of a ringed binder. "I'm Captain Sean Webb. I worked closely with search efforts. We understand that you were followed by two or more men who we think are responsible for multiple murders in the area."

"Yes, I found someone. A body. Moxie must have picked up the scent of him and led me there. My guide dog. They came for me and I had to run. I think they shot her."

"Can you tell me how many there were?"

"Three of them, at least."

He circles something and the gimbaled feet of his chair squeal as he balances on the rear legs, then he breathes. "Here's where I ask if there's anything about the men you could possibly identify. Did you, for instance, hear any of their voices?"

"I did."

"Okay, that's good. If we find the last man I'd like to play samples of his voice to determine if you can pick him out. Like an auditory lineup, if you will."

"You found the others?"

"Alive, for the moment, we found a man named Glen Stalls. He looked like he was making his way around Little Bass to you. Since he never planned on being taken alive he opened fire on police and was wounded in the exchange. We don't expect him to make it. Dead, we found a man named Tanner Wilson in a burnt out cabin four miles from Little Bass."

"I remember him. He gave me his name."

"You spoke with him?"

"I took his rifle from him."

He sets the chair back down on all its legs and I think he leans in to get a better look at my eyes; his voice is close when he says, "Jessica tells us you're totally blind."

"She tells the truth," I say. "Tanner was dead when you found him?"

"Shot in the chest and the body burned. We think they killed him in some attempt to stall us. It worked, for a little while. As for the last man we're at a loss. It looks like he might have gone north from Little Bass but where after is anyone's guess."

"His name is Frank," I say. "I went to school and to camp with him. I don't have a last name for you."

"What can you tell me about him?"

"He had scoliosis when I knew him. Scars on his knuckles."

The Captain asks for more basic information, such as age and race, and I answer. "Very good. We shouldn't have trouble finding him with all that. But, I'll need to know how you came to know it was him? His inevitable defense will be that you're blind, and there's no way you could identify him."

I tell him what I heard him say to me at the old river bed many years past and what he said to me on the bridge only days ago. He jots it down. "Will it be enough?" I ask.

"To bring him in? Of course. To put him away? I doubt it, but that's alright. As long as we have the man to connect physical evidence to we'll pin the bastard eventually." The Captain breathes again. "But there's much more I need to ask you about, Avery."

"There's more I need to tell," I say, and before he can ask I tell him everything. It comes out unorganized and in reverse. In order of importance, I suppose. I tell him that the man named Daniel McLloyd tricked me into helping him hide the body of someone he'd killed, and that he must have done the very same with Frank, and that Frank must have taken to killing. I tell him what I did to Daniel and where. "I'll walk you through every blow. Exactly where the ax hit the floorboards," I say. "It happened just as I remember. But when my father told me that what I remember couldn't be true I kept it to myself. I wish I didn't do that."

The Captain is silent but for the lashing of his pen on the notepad. Eventually he says, "I'm not so sure. Suppose you told the police. Even if they believed you, nothing you'd have told them could have stopped what came. You didn't know about Frank. None of this is your fault."

"I won't have you take my guilt from me," I tell him. I think he smiles. "But I still struggle with how their bodies turned up at Burntside? I can't imagine Frank would have thought to do that."

"No, he wouldn't have done that," he says, then clears his throat. "Did you ever meet a man named Aaron McLloyd?"

"I don't believe so. But I learned Daniel had an older brother."

"That's right. At the time he was a detective, and he was Chief of Police until resigning just yesterday. This remains to be proven, but I believe he had something to do with it. He told me that he found you on that Promontory those years ago. He said we'd find you there again. You were air-lifted here yesterday morning. Can you remember any of that? The first time, I mean."

"It's difficult. I was delirious. It's like a dream. I think I was carried off... I must have been."

"That's fine." The man lets out a breath and stands. "That'll be all for now. Rest. We'll continue later."

"Tell me," I say. "I won't sleep until I understand."

"You're in good company then. I've spent all night trying to figure it myself. Maybe Aaron is waiting to tell it to you first. Maybe that's all it is. So rest, as best you can."

But it's no feat of imagination to figure it: Daniel had it in his mind to prove that whatever he had become everyone else was one step from becoming themselves. He had shown me, Frank, and his own brother the things he'd been up to. He'd picked us because we were wounded like him. Frank had taken to it, persuaded by Daniel to make everyone his victim as revenge for being born the way he was. Aaron was no killer though, having saved me, but he must have protected his brother in some way. Helped conceal evidence. He must have understood that if his brother was revealed as the killer it would have brought an investigation into himself, so he worked to make it look like Daniel was just another victim along with the others.

As for me, I ran out of fear and no more, but that's good enough.

"I almost forgot," says the Captain. "Aaron wanted me to give you this." He pulls at a zipper and takes something from his binder and falls silent, studying whatever he now holds. "It's been sitting in his office since I can remember," he says. "I'd describe it to you, but it would only fall short." The Captain places it on the metal tray next to my gurney. I reach out and take it up it in my hand. "What does it mean?" he asks.

I don't answer. Reluctant or unable to. It's an acknowledgment of a shared past. The Cecropia was an adopted fixation. In truth Lily was scared of bugs – of so many things – but maybe this was her first exception. A start onto finding virtue in what frightened her. I'd like to think she was further along than those who live a hundred years and pass unpersuaded after all.

Captain Webb says his farewells and leaves as quietly as he came in.

The Cecropia in its acrylic dome once spanned the circumference of my hand. It feels smaller there now, but hasn't diminished in memory, and it shines under a golden light from a low sun always setting or always rising. The crimson accents just before the outer margins catch the light like cinders burning in the depths of ashen coal. The blue-gray eye spots at the wing ends are the like of its most pursuant predator. They are owl's eyes.

When Jessica returns she doesn't ask about it. Not at first. She only remarks how it looks in the sun through the window. When she speaks the light assumes no form. It doesn't put her there as someone else. After long she sits and asks where it fits in the cabin at Burntside. I tell her it wasn't mine for long and can go anywhere.

Acknowledgments

This novel is an adaptation of a screenplay I wrote in 2011 under the title "Beacons." I wasn't serious about writing then, and never expected to be offered representation by a literary management company. My contract with that company fell through after 2 years, but the experience, along with encouragement from family and friends, convinced me that maybe I should take writing seriously. There have been a few players who might not take credit themselves, but whose contributions helped bring this work to life. Teachers of mine who pulled me aside to tell me to keep writing. My Father, urging me on and even helping with rewrites for the screenplay because he believed in the idea after I had abandoned it. (Alas, I abandoned it again for many years, but all the same.) I'd also like to thank Damian Modena, who did an amazing job with the cover illustration for this edition, and Eric W, who proofread it.

Anyway, I'll end by saying that to write anything, you need to be a bit foolish. You need to play a kind of trick on yourself that one day it'll lead to something worthwhile. But this only goes so far. You need some notion that it's true, and that only comes from others.

To those who gave me that, thank you.